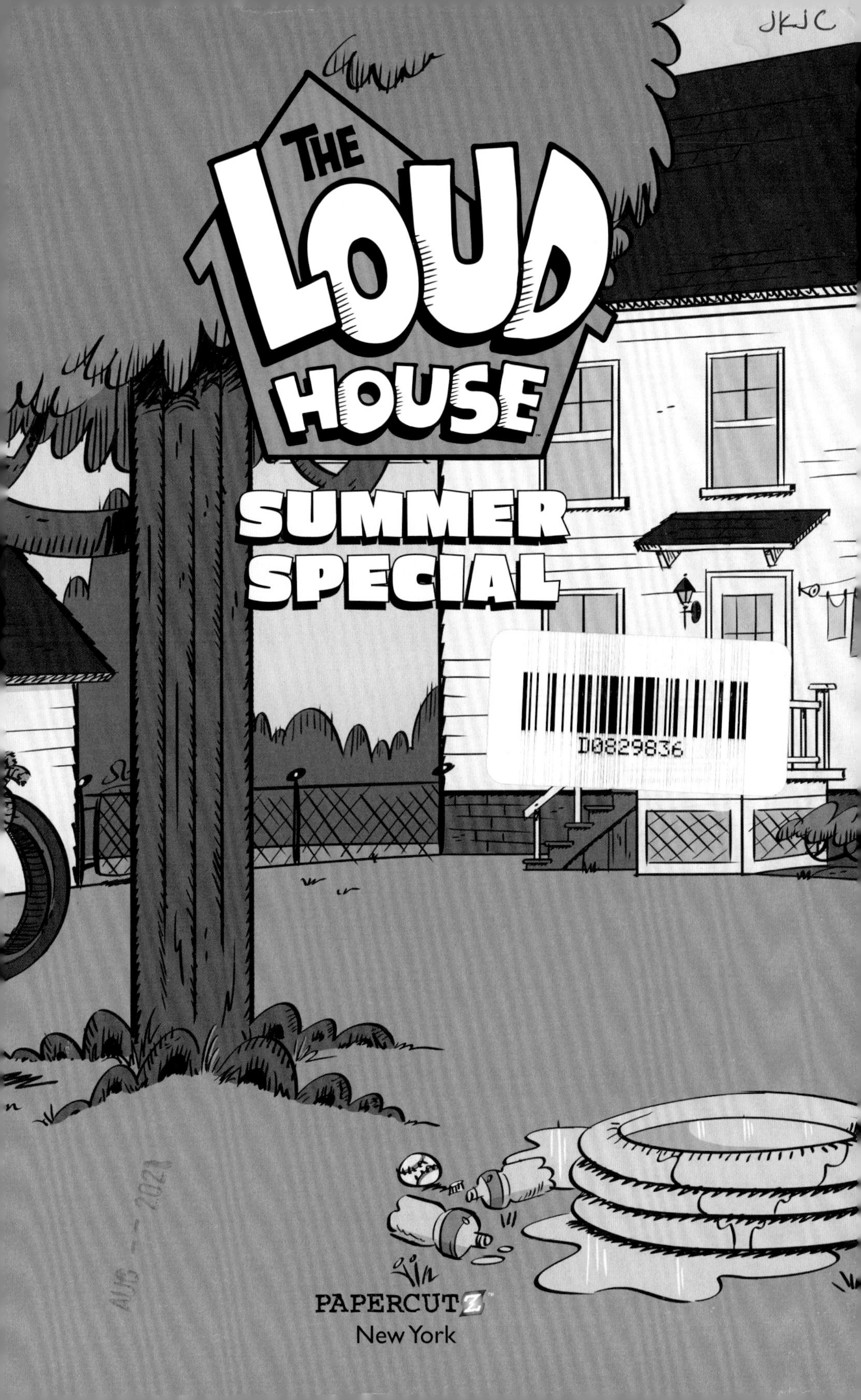

The Loud House
Summer Special

PAPERCUTZ
New York

nickelodeon GRAPHIC NOVELS AVAILABLE FROM PAPERCUTZ

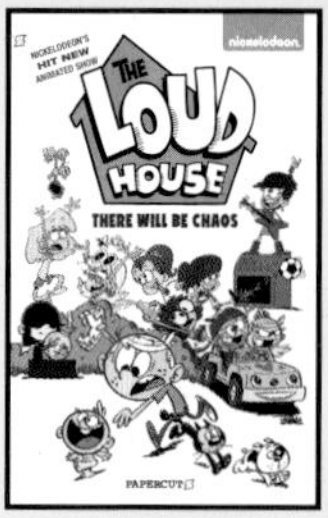
THE LOUD HOUSE
THERE WILL BE CHAOS

THE LOUD HOUSE
#1
"There Will Be Chaos"

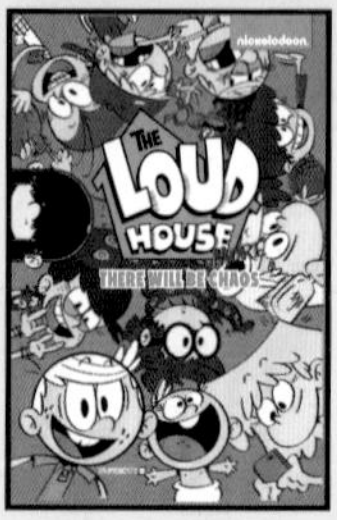
THE LOUD HOUSE

THE LOUD HOUSE
#2
"There Will Be More Chaos"

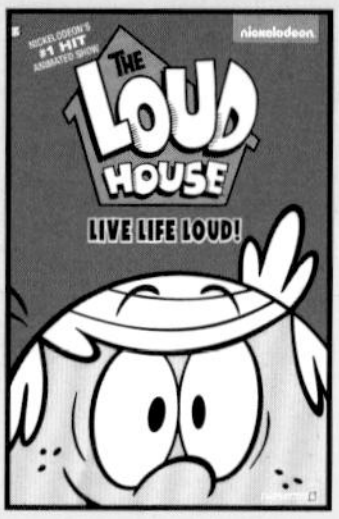
THE LOUD HOUSE
LIVE LIFE LOUD!

THE LOUD HOUSE
#3
"Live Life Loud!"

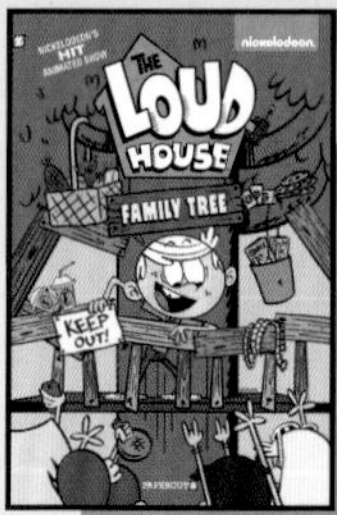
THE LOUD HOUSE
FAMILY TREE
KEEP OUT!

THE LOUD HOUSE
#4
"Family Tree"

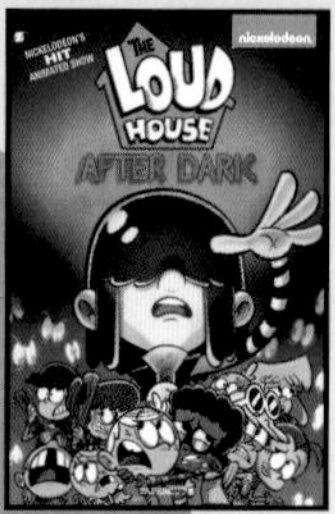
THE LOUD HOUSE
AFTER DARK

THE LOUD HOUSE
#5
"After Dark"

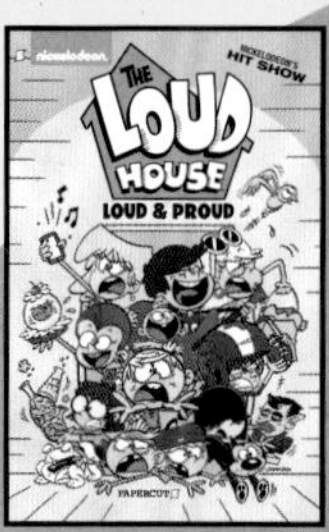
THE LOUD HOUSE
LOUD & PROUD

THE LOUD HOUSE
#6
"Loud and Proud"

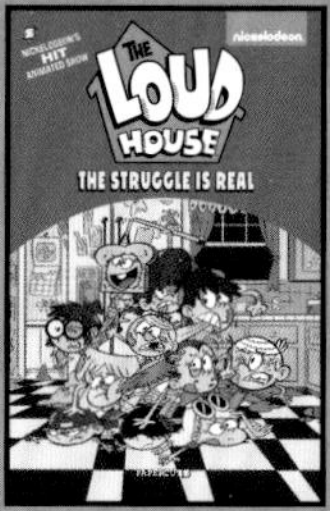
THE LOUD HOUSE
THE STRUGGLE IS REAL

THE LOUD HOUSE
#7
"The Struggle is Real"

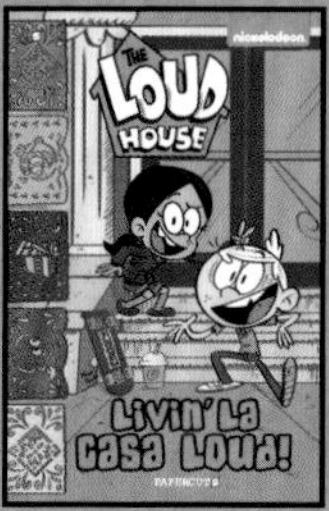
THE LOUD HOUSE
Livin' La Casa Loud!

THE LOUD HOUSE
#8
"Livin' La Casa Loud"

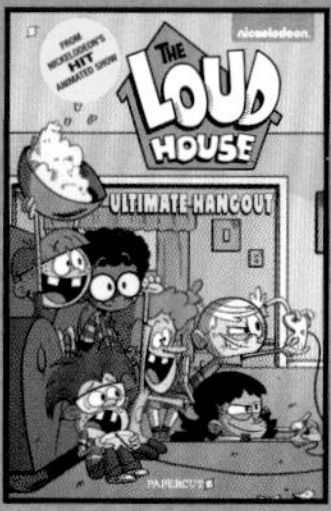
THE LOUD HOUSE
ULTIMATE HANGOUT

THE LOUD HOUSE
#9
"Ultimate Hangout"

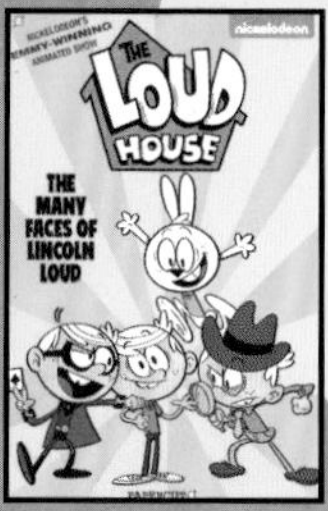
THE LOUD HOUSE
THE MANY FACES OF LINCOLN LOUD

THE LOUD HOUSE
#10
"The Many Faces of Lincoln Loud"

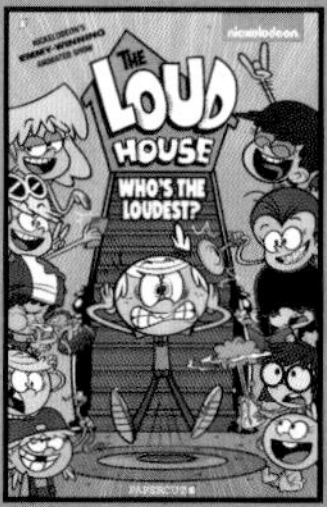
THE LOUD HOUSE
WHO'S THE LOUDEST?

THE LOUD HOUSE
#11
"Who's the Loudest?"

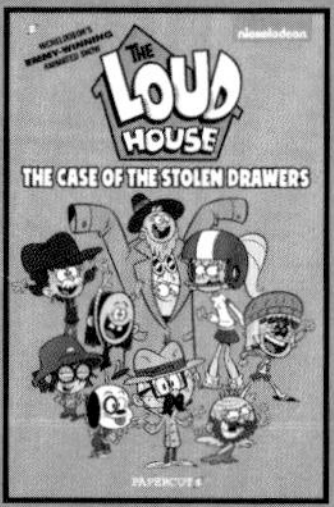
THE LOUD HOUSE
THE CASE OF THE STOLEN DRAWERS

THE LOUD HOUSE
#12
"The Case of the Stolen Drawers"

COMING SOON

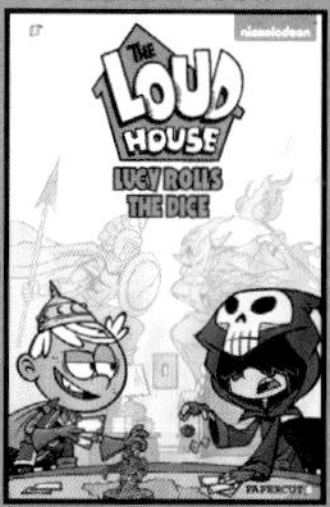
THE LOUD HOUSE
LUCY ROLLS THE DICE

THE LOUD HOUSE
#13
"Lucy Rolls the Dice"

COMING SOON

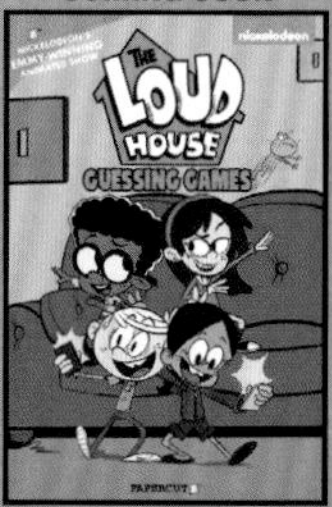
THE LOUD HOUSE
GUESSING GAMES

THE LOUD HOUSE
#14
"Guessing Games"

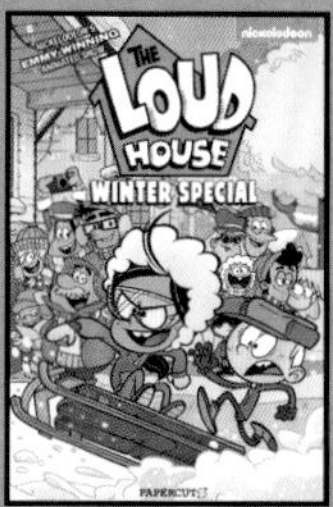
THE LOUD HOUSE
WINTER SPECIAL

THE LOUD HOUSE
WINTER SPECIAL

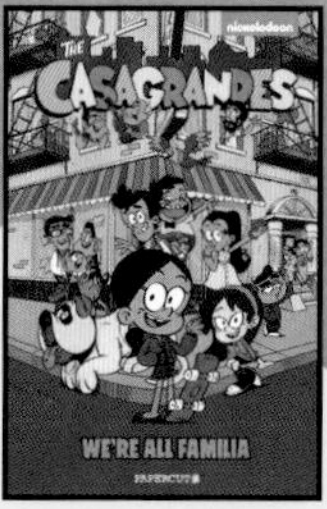
THE CASAGRANDES
WE'RE ALL FAMILIA

THE CASAGRANDES
SPECIAL

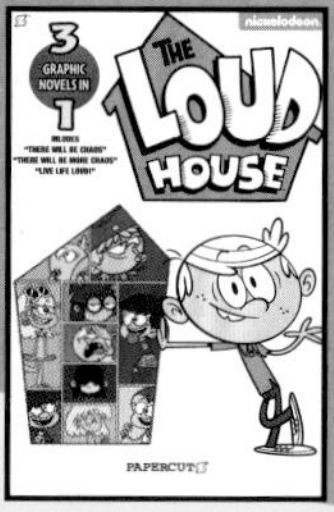
3 GRAPHIC NOVELS IN 1
THE LOUD HOUSE

THE LOUD HOUSE
3 IN 1
#1

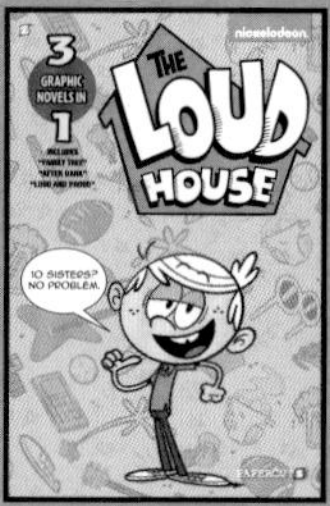
3 GRAPHIC NOVELS IN 1
THE LOUD HOUSE
10 SISTERS? NO PROBLEM.

THE LOUD HOUSE
3 IN 1
#2

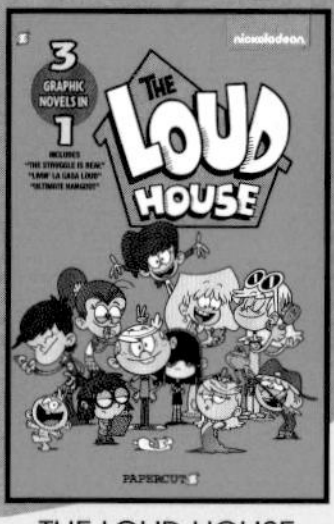
3 GRAPHIC NOVELS IN 1
THE LOUD HOUSE

THE LOUD HOUSE
3 IN 1
#3

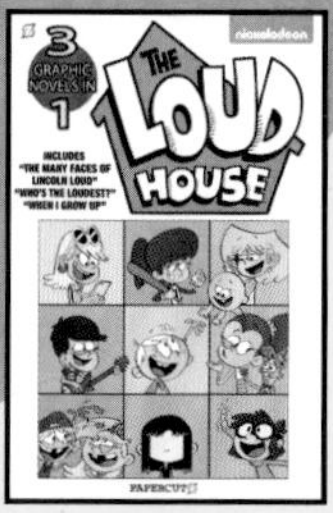
3 GRAPHIC NOVELS IN 1
THE LOUD HOUSE

THE LOUD HOUSE
3 IN 1
#4

The Loud House and The Casagrandes graphic novels and specials are available for $7.99 each in paperback, $12.99 each in hardcover. THE LOUD HOUSE 3 IN 1 graphic novels are available for $14.99 each in paperback only. Available from booksellers everywhere. You can also order online from Papercutz.com, or call 1-800-886-1223, Monday through Friday, 9-5 EST. MC, Visa, and AmEx accepted. To order by mail, please add $5.00 for postage and handling for the first book ordered, $1.00 for each additional book and make check payable to NBM Publishing. Send to: Papercutz, 160 Broadway, Suite 700, East Wing, New York, NY 10038.

Nickelodeon graphic novels are also available digitally wherever e-books are sold.

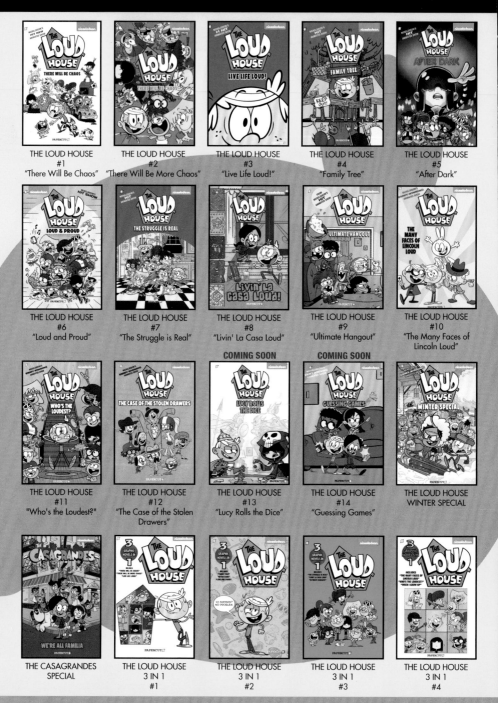

THE LOUD HOUSE

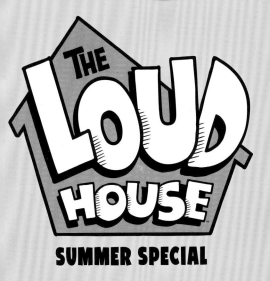

SUMMER SPECIAL

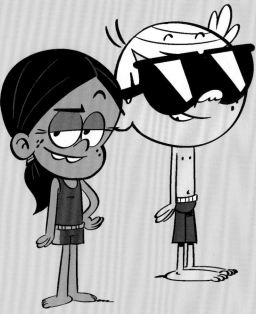

nickelodeon™ THE LOUD HOUSE

SUMMER SPECIAL

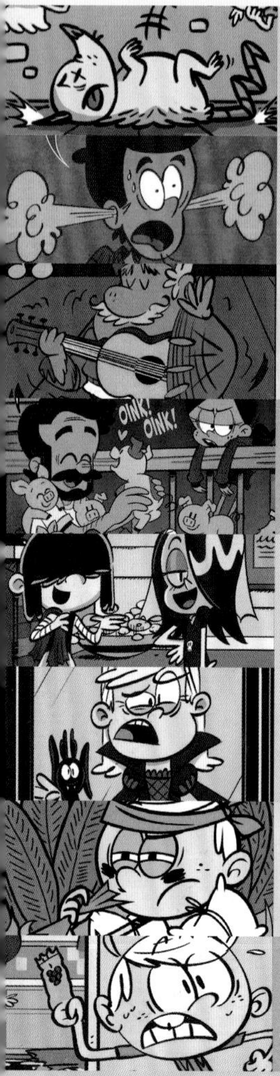

OINK! OINK!

"O POSSUM, WHERE ART THOU?"
Caitlin Fein — Writer
Isaiah Kim — Artist
Peter Bertucci — Colorist
Wilson Ramos Jr. — Letterer

"EVEN THE SCORE"
Hannah Watanabe-Rocco — Writer
Zazo Aguiar — Artist, Colorist
Karolyne Rocha — Inker
Vic Miyuki — Colorist
Wilson Ramos Jr. — Letterer

"BOBBY IN DISTRESS"
Julia Rothenbuhler-Garcia — Writer
Jose Hernandez — Artist, Colorist
Wilson Ramos Jr. — Letterer

"TUNNEL OF MUD"
Hannah Watanabe-Rocco — Writer
Daniela Rodriguez — Artist, Colorist
Wilson Ramos Jr. — Letterer

"WE WILL ROCK YOU"
Kristen G. Smith — Writer
Way Singleton — Artist
Efrain Rodriguez — Colorist
Wilson Ramos Jr. — Letterer

"LUNCH ON THE RUN"
Kristen G. Smith — Writer
Tyler Koberstein — Artist, Colorist
Wilson Ramos Jr. — Letterer

"WHAT GOES UP"
Kristen G. Smith — Writer
Jennifer Hernandez — Artist, Colorist
Wilson Ramos Jr. — Letterer

"SUNDAY IN THE PARK"
Kristen G. Smith — Writer
Erin Hunting — Artist, Colorist
Wilson Ramos Jr. — Letterer

"LUCY'S SUMMER FASHION TIPS"
Caitlin Fein — Writer
Max Alley — Artist
Peter Bertucci — Colorist
Wilson Ramos Jr. — Letterer

"ONE LOUD'S TRASH"
Caitlin Fein — Writer
Ron Bradley — Artist, Colorist
Wilson Ramos Jr. — Letterer

"DOOM AND BLOOM"
Jair Holguin — Writer
Max Alley — Artist
Peter Bertucci — Colorist
Wilson Ramos Jr. — Letterer

"PREP TALK"
Derek Fridolfs — Writer
Angela Zhang — Artist
Ronda Pattison — Colorist
Wilson Ramos Jr. — Letterer

"LINCOLN'S SURVIVAL GUIDE"
Jair Holguin — Writer
Melissa Kleynowski —Penciler
Zazo Aguiar — Inker
Vic Miyuki — Colorist
Wilson Ramos Jr. — Letterer

"CASA CAMPERS"
Kristen G. Smith — Writer
Kelsey Wooley — Artist, Colorist
Wilson Ramos Jr. — Letterer

"POPSICLE PROBLEMS"
Kevin Sullivan — Writer
Diem Doan — Artist, Colorist, Letterer

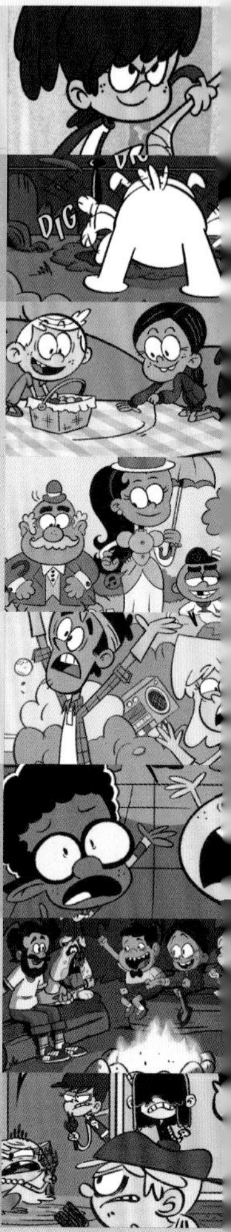

DIG

JORDAN ROSATO — Endpapers
JAMES SALERNO — Sr. Art Director/Nickelodeon
JAYJAY JACKSON — Design
EMMA BONE, CAITLIN FEIN, KRISTEN G. SMITH, NEIL WADE, DANA CLUVERIUS, MOLLIE FREILICH — Special Thanks
JEFF WHITMAN — Editor
INGRID RIOS — Editorial Intern
JOAN HILTY — Comics Editor/Nickelodeon
JIM SALICRUP
Editor-in-Chief

ISBN: 978-1-5458-0692-0 paperback edition
ISBN: 978-1-5458-0691-3 hardcover edition

www.papercutz.com

Papercutz books may be purchased for business or promotional use. For information on bulk purchases please contact Macmillan Corporate and Premium Sales Department at (800) 221-7945 x5442.

Printed in Turkey
June 2021

Distributed by Macmillan
First Printing

MEET THE LOUD FAMILY *and friends!*

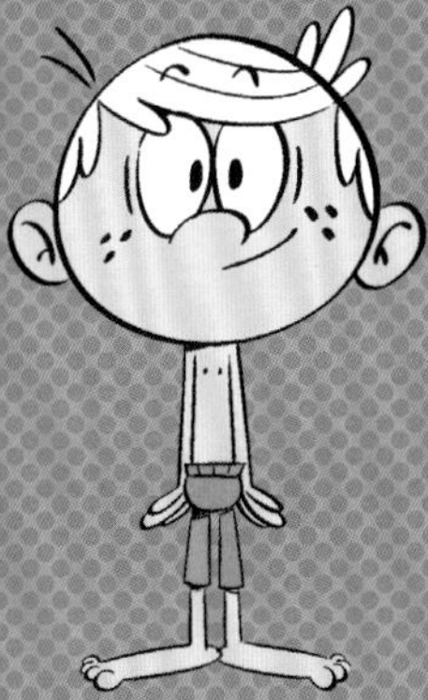

LINCOLN LOUD
THE MIDDLE CHILD

Lincoln is the middle child, with five older sisters and five younger sisters. He has learned that surviving the Loud household means staying a step ahead. He's the man with a plan, always coming up with a way to get what he wants or deal with a problem, even if things inevitably go wrong. Being the only boy comes with some perks. Lincoln gets his own room – even if it's just a converted linen closet. On the other hand, being the only boy also means he sometimes gets a little too much attention from his sisters. They mother him, tease him, and use him as the occasional lab rat or fashion show participant. Lincoln's sisters may drive him crazy, but he loves them and is always willing to help out if they need him.

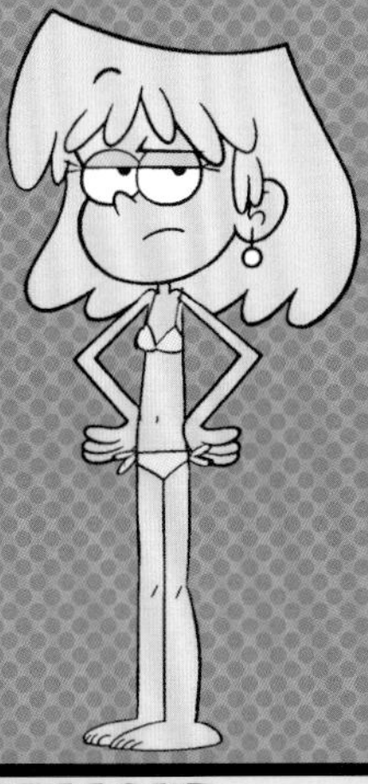

LORI LOUD
THE OLDEST

As the first-born child of the Loud Clan, Lori sees herself as the boss of all her siblings. She feels she's paved the way for them and deserves extra respect. Her signature traits are rolling her eyes, texting her boyfriend, Bobby, and literally saying "literally" all the time. Because she's the oldest and most experienced sibling, Lori can be a great ally, so it pays to stay on her good side, especially since she can drive.

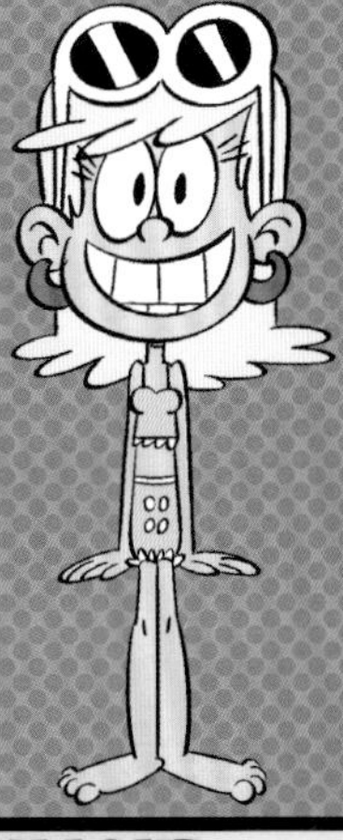

LENI LOUD
THE FASHIONISTA

Leni spends most of her time designing outfits and accessorizing. She always falls for Luan's pranks, and sometimes walks into walls when she's talking (she's not great at doing two things at once). Leni might be flighty, but she's the sweetest of the Loud siblings and truly has a heart of gold (even though she's pretty sure it's a heart of blood).

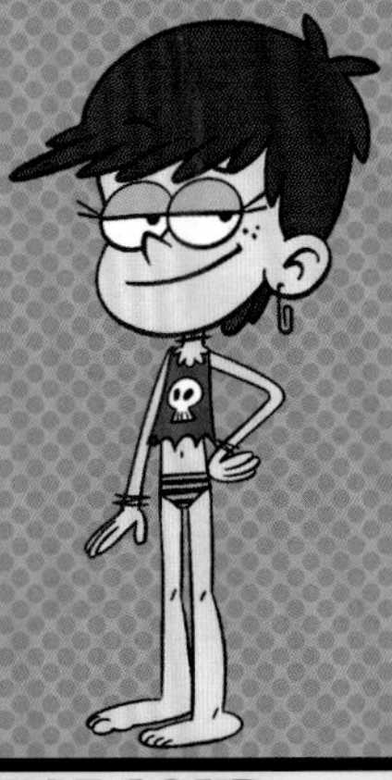

LUNA LOUD
THE ROCK STAR

Luna is loud, boisterous, freewheeling, and her energy is always cranked to 11. She thinks about music so much that she even talks in song lyrics. On the off-chance she doesn't have her guitar with her, everything can and will be turned into a musical instrument. You can always count on Luna to help out, and she'll do most anything you ask, as long as you're okay with her supplying a rocking guitar accompaniment.

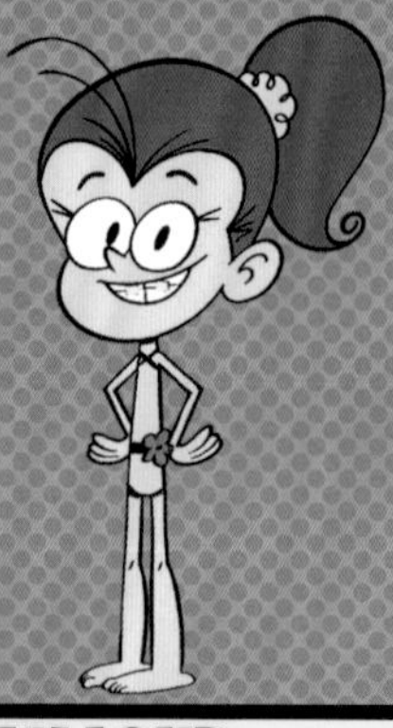

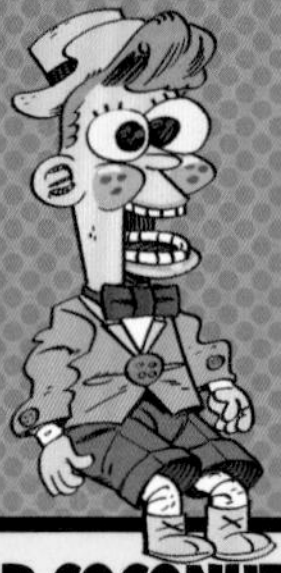

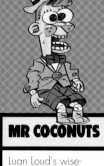

MR COCONUTS

Luan Loud's wise-cracking dummy.

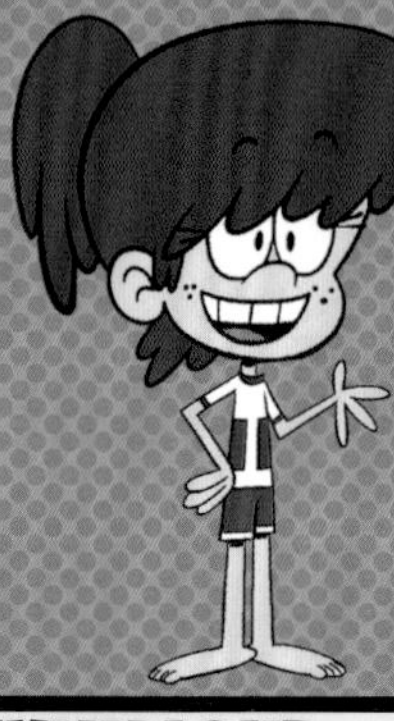

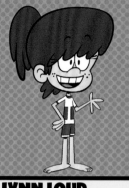

LUAN LOUD
THE JOKESTER

Luan's a standup comedienne who provides a nonstop barrage of silly puns. She's big on prop comedy too – squirting flowers and whoopee cushions – so you have to be on your toes whenever she's around. She loves to pull pranks and is a really good ventriloquist – she is often found doing bits with her dummy, Mr. Coconuts. Luan never lets anything get her down; to her, laughter IS the best medicine.

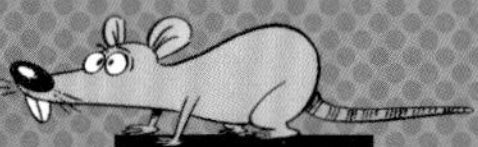

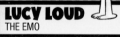

BITEY

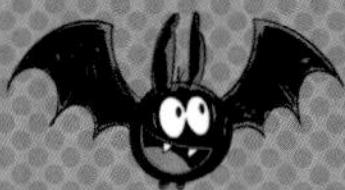

FANGS

LYNN LOUD
THE ATHLETE

Lynn is athletic and full of energy and is always looking for a teammate. With her, it's all sports all the time. She'll turn anything into a sport. Putting away eggs? Jump shot! Score! Cleaning up the eggs? Slap shot! Score! Lynn is very competitive, but despite her competitive nature, she always tries to just have a good time.

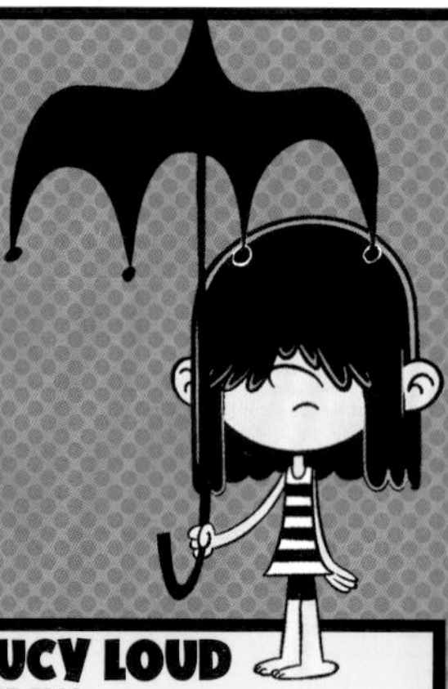

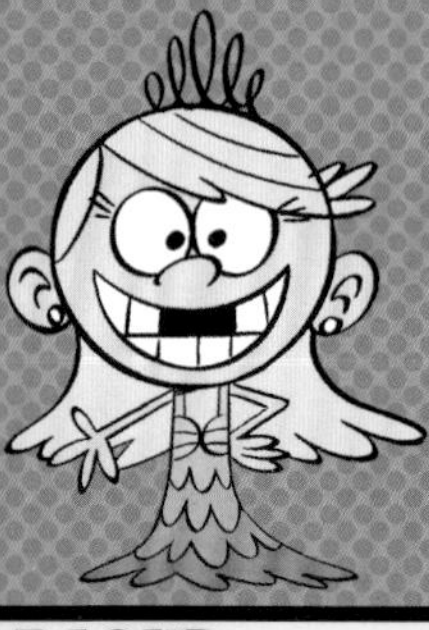

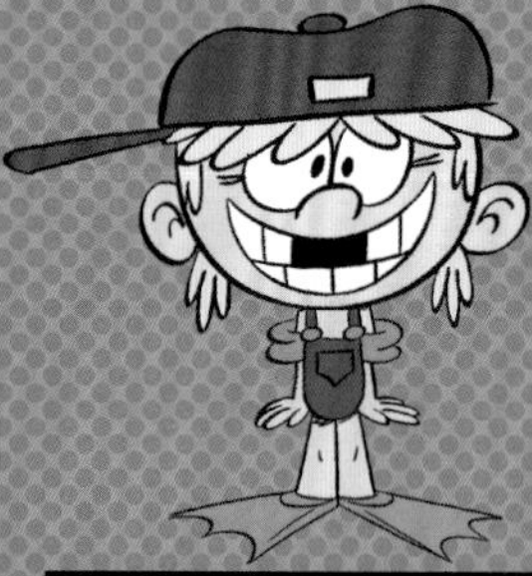

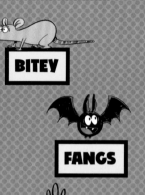

LUCY LOUD
THE EMO

You can always count on Lucy to give the morbid point of view in any given situation. She is obsessed with all things spooky and dark – funerals, vampires, séances, and the like. She wears mostly black and writes moody poetry. She's usually quiet and keeps to herself. Lucy has a way of mysteriously appearing out of nowhere, and try as they might, her siblings never get used to this.

LOLA LOUD
THE BEAUTY QUEEN

Lola could not be more different from her twin sister, Lana. She's a pageant powerhouse whose interests include glitter, photo shoots, and her own beautiful, beautiful face. But don't let her cute, gap-toothed smile fool you; underneath all the sugar and spice lurks a Machiavellian mastermind. Whatever Lola wants, Lola gets – or else. She's the eyes and ears of the household and never resists an opportunity to tattle on troublemakers. But if you stay on Lola's good side, you've got yourself a fierce ally – and a lifetime supply of free makeovers.

LANA LOUD
THE TOMBOY

Lana is the rough-and-tumble sparkplug counterpart to her twin sister, Lola. She's all about reptiles, mud pies, and muffler repair. She's the resident Ms. Fix-it and is always ready to lend a hand – the dirtier the job, the better. Need your toilet unclogged? Snake fed? Back-zit popped? Lana's your gal. All she asks in return is a little A-B-C gum, or a handful of kibble (she often sneaks it from the dog bowl).

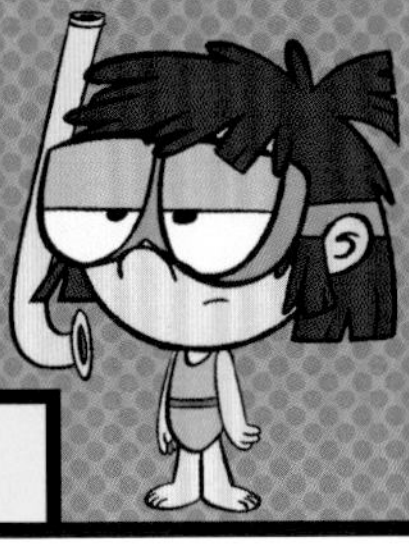

LISA LOUD
THE GENIUS

Lisa is smarter than the rest of her siblings combined. She'll most likely be a rocket scientist, or a brain surgeon, or an evil genius who takes over the world. Lisa spends most of her time working in her lab (the family has gotten used to the explosions), and says her research leaves little time for frivolous human pursuits like "playing" or "getting haircuts." That said, she's always there to help with a homework question, or to explain why the sky is blue, or to point out the structural flaws in someone's pillow fort. Lisa says it's the least she can do for her favorite test subjects, er, siblings.

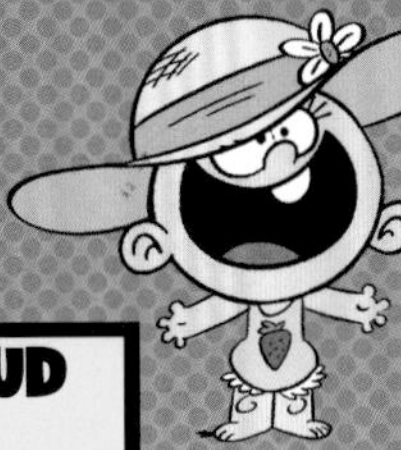

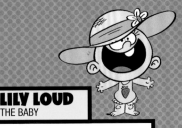

LILY LOUD
THE BABY

Lily is a giggly, drooly, diaper-ditching free spirit, affectionately known as "the poop machine." You can't keep a nappy on this kid – she's like a teething Houdini. But even when Lily's running wild, dropping rancid diaper bombs, or drooling all over the remote, she always brings a smile to everyone's face (and a clothespin to their nose). Lily is everyone's favorite little buddy, and the whole family loves her unconditionally.

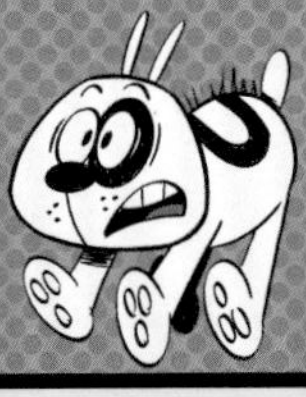

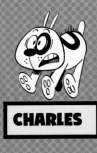

CHARLES

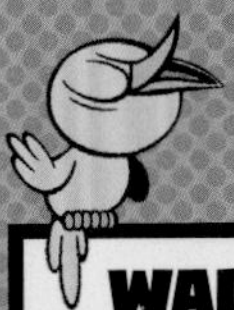

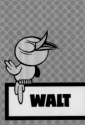

WALT

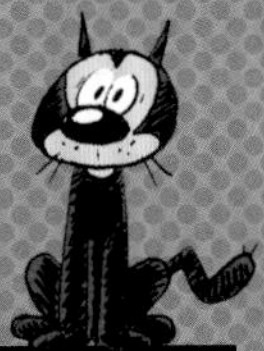

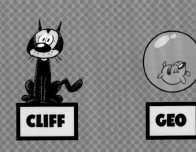

CLIFF

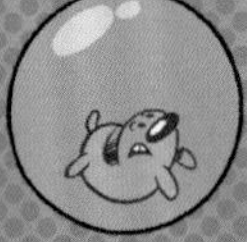

GEO

RITA LOUD

Mother to the eleven Loud kids, Mom (Rita Loud) wears many different hats. She's a chauffeur, homework-checker, and barf-cleaner-upper all rolled into one. She's always there for her kids and ready to jump into action during a crisis, whether it's a fight between the twins or Leni's missing shoe. When she's not chasing the kids around or at her day job as a dental hygienist, Mom pursues her passion: writing. She also loves taking on house projects and is very handy with tools (guess that's where Lana gets it from). Between writing, working, and being a mom, her days are always hectic but she wouldn't have it any other way.

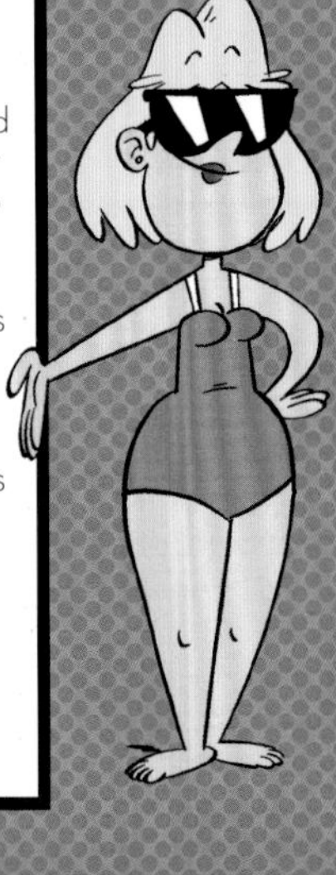

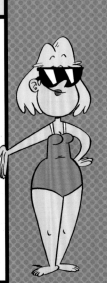

LYNN LOUD SR.

Dad (Lynn Loud Sr.) is a fun-loving, upbeat aspiring chef. A kid-at-heart, he's not above taking part in the kids' zany schemes. In addition to cooking, Dad loves his van, playing the cowbell. and making puns. Before meeting Mom, Dad spent a semester in England and has been obsessed with British culture ever since – and sometimes "accidentally" slips into a British accent. When Dad's not wrangling the kids, he's pursuing his dream of opening his own restaurant where he hopes to make his "Lynn-sagnas" world-famous.

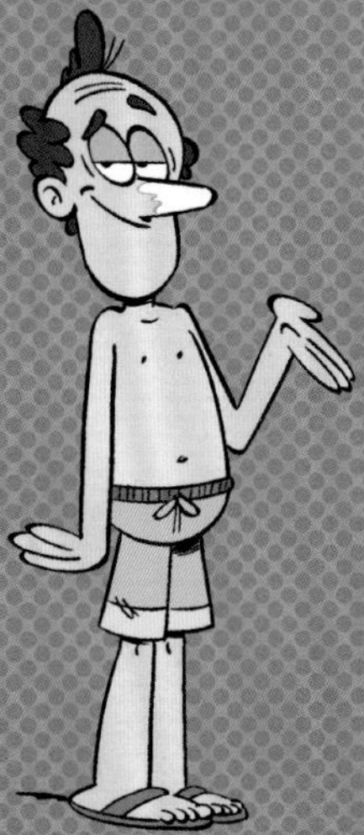

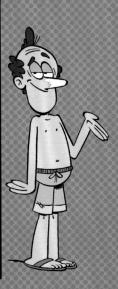

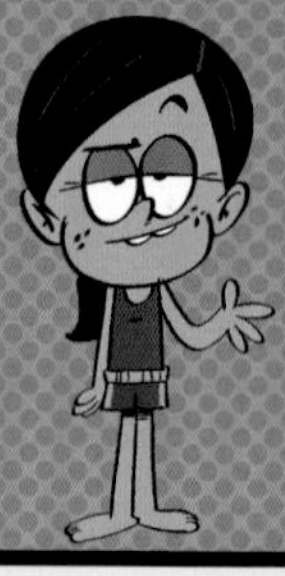

RONNIE ANNE SANTIAGO

Ronnie Anne's a skateboarding city girl now. She's fearless, free-spirited, and always quick to come up with a plan. She's one tough cookie, but she also has a sweet side. Ronnie Anne loves helping her family, and that's taught her to help others, too. When she's not pitching in at the family mercado, you can find her exploring the neighborhood with her best friend Sid, or ordering hot dogs with her skater buds Casey, Nikki, and Sameer.

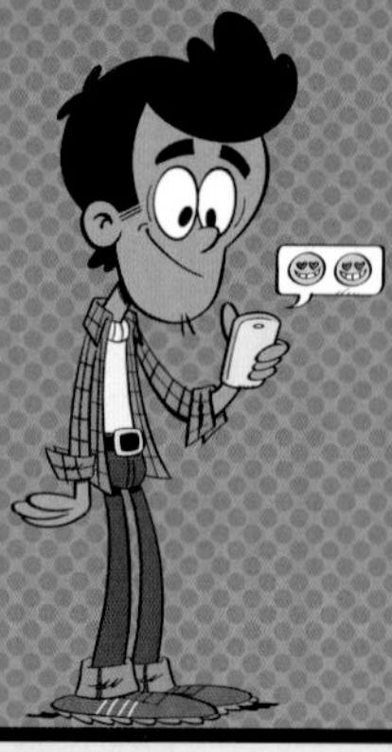

BOBBY SANTIAGO

Bobby is Ronnie Anne's big bro. He's a student and one of the hardest workers in the city! He loves his family and loves working at the Mercado. As his Abuelo's right hand man, Bobby can't wait to take over the family business one day. He's a big kid at heart, and his clumsiness gets him into some sticky situations at work, like locking himself in the freezer. Mercado mishaps aside, everyone in the neighborhood loves to come to the store and talk to Bobby.

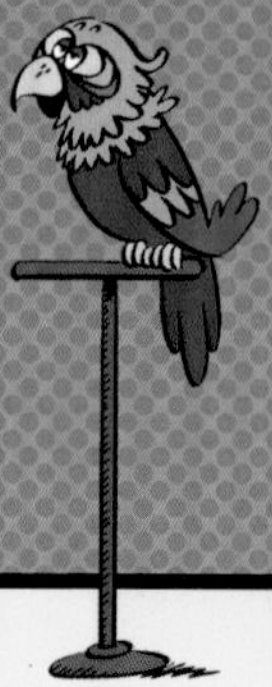

SERGIO

Sergio is the Casagrandes' beloved pet parrot. He's a blunt, sassy bird who "thinks" he's full of wisdom, and always has something to say. The Casagrandes have to keep a close eye on their credit card as Sergio is addicted to online shopping and is always asking the family to buy him some new gadget he saw on TV. Sergio is most loyal to Rosa and serves as her wing-man, partner in crime, taste tester, and confidant. Sergio is quite popular in the neighborhood and is always up for a good time.

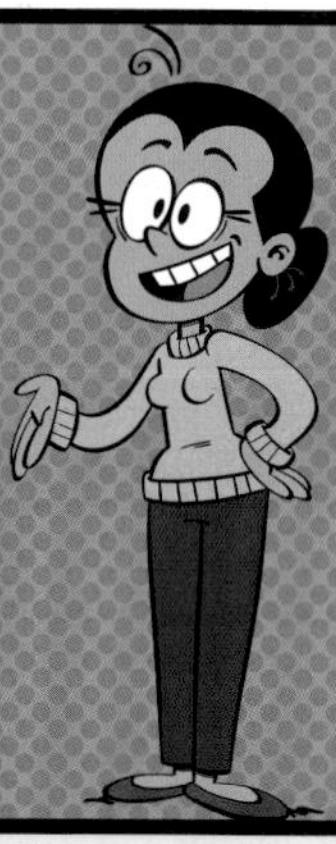

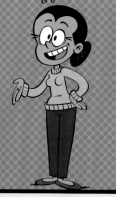

MARIA CASAGRANDE SANTIAGO

She's the mother of Bobby and Ronnie Anne. A hardworking nurse, she doesn't get to spend a lot of time with her kids, but when she does she treasures it. Maria is calm and rational but often worries about whether she's doing enough for her kids. Maria, Bobby, and Ronnie Anne are a close-knit trio who were used to having only each other – until they moved in with their extended family.

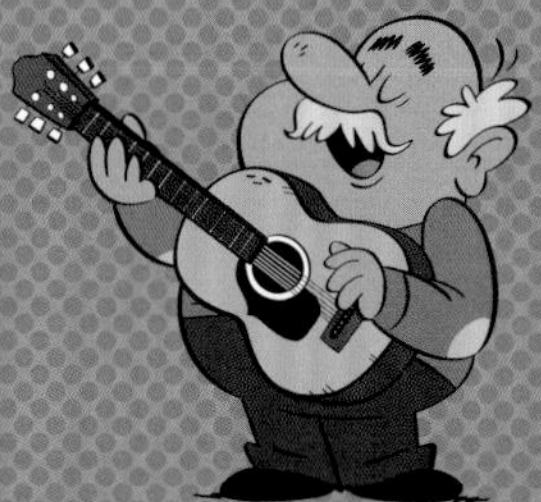

HECTOR CASAGRANDE

Hector is Carlos and Maria's dad, and the Abuelo of the family (that means grandpa)! He owns the Mercado on the ground floor of their apartment building and takes great pride in his work, his family, and being the unofficial "mayor" of the block. He loves to tell stories, share his ideas, and gossip (even though he won't admit to it). You can find him working in the Mercado, playing guitar, or watching his favorite telenovela.

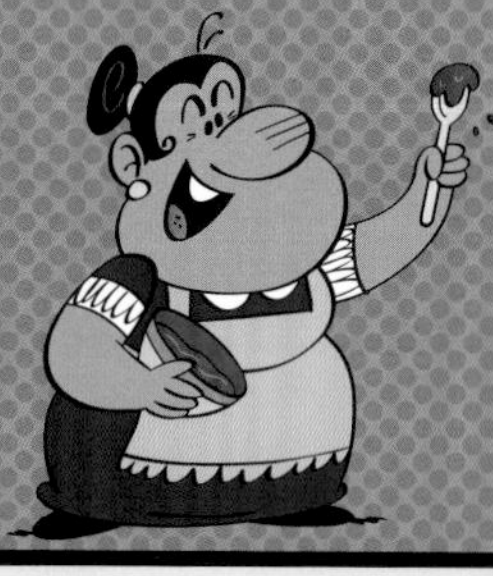

ROSA CASAGRANDE

Rosa is Carlos and Maria's mom and the Abuela of the family (that means grandma)! She's the head of the household, the wisest Casagrande, and the master cook with a superhuman ability to tell when anyone in the house is hungry. She often tries to fix problems or illnesses with traditional Mexican home remedies and potions. She's very protective of her family… sometimes a little too much.

CARLOS CASAGRANDE

Carlos is Maria's brother. He's married to Frida, and together they have four kids: Carlota, C.J., Carl, and Carlitos. Carlos is a Professor of Cultural Studies at a local college. Usually he has his heads in the clouds or his nose in a textbook. Relatively easygoing, Carlos is a loving father and an enthusiastic teacher who tries to get his kids interested in their Mexican heritage.

FRIDA PUGA CASAGRANDE

Frida is Carlos, C.J., Carl, and Carlitos' mom. She's an art professor and a performance artist, and is always looking for new ways to express herself. She's got a big heart and isn't shy about her emotions. Frida tends to cry when she's sad, happy, angry, or any other emotion you can think of. She's always up for fun, is passionate about her art, and loves her family more than anything.

CARLOTA CASAGRANDE

Carlota is CJ, Carl, and Carlitos' older sister. A social media influencer, she's excited to be like a big sister to Ronnie Anne. She's a force to be reckoned with, and is always trying to share her distinctive vintage style tips with Ronnie Anne.

CJ (CARLOS JR.) CASAGRANDE

CJ is Carlota's younger brother and Carl and Carlitos' older brother. He was born with Down Syndrome. He lights up any room with his infectious smile and is always ready to play. He's obsessed with pirates and is BFFs with Bobby. He likes to wear a bowtie to any family occasion, and you can always catch him laughing or helping his *abuela*.

CARL CASAGRANDE

Carl is wise beyond his years. He's confident, outgoing, and puts a lot of time and effort into looking good. He likes to think of himself as a suave businessman and doesn't like to get caught playing with his action figures or wearing his footie PJs. Even though Bobby is nothing but nice to him, Carl sees his big cousin as his biggest rival.

CARLITOS CASAGRANDE

Carlitos is the baby of the family, and is always copying the behavior of everyone in the household—even if they aren't human. He's a playful and silly baby who loves to play with the family pets.

LALO

Lalo is a slobbery bull mastiff who thinks he's a lapdog. He's not the smartest pup, and gets scared easily… but he loves his family and loves to cuddle.

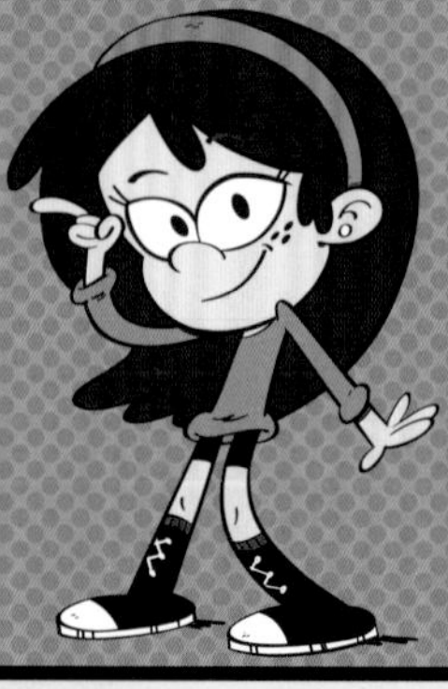

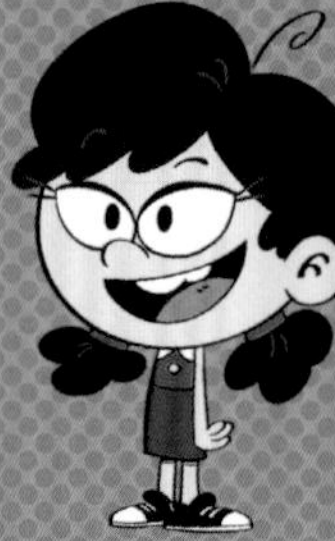

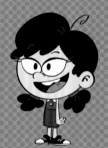

SID CHANG

Sid is Ronnie Anne's quirky best friend. She's new to the city but dives head-first into everything she finds interesting. She and her family just moved into the apartment one floor above the Casagrandes. In fact, Sid's bedroom is right above Ronnie Anne's! A dream come true for any BFFs.

ADELAIDE CHANG

Adelaide Chang is Sid's little sister. She's 6 years old, and has a flair for the dramatic. You can always find her trying to make her way into her big sister Sid's adventures.

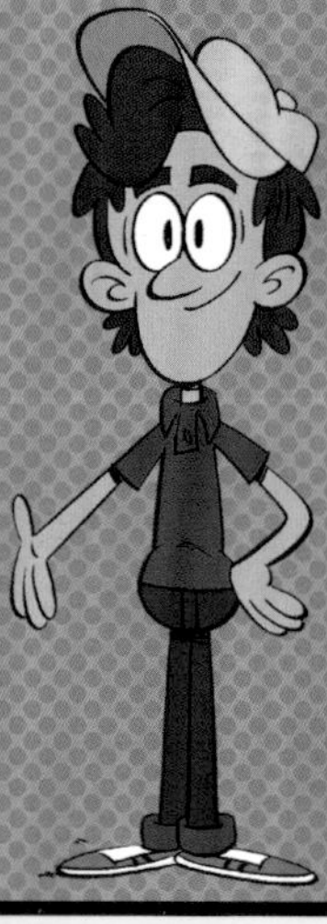

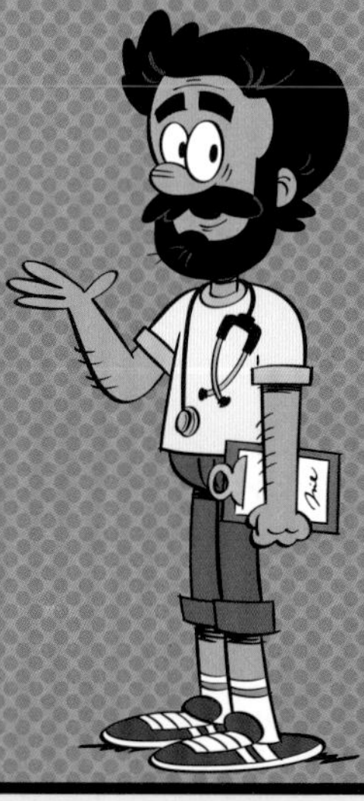

PAR

Par is the *Mercado's* produce delivery guy. He's an outgoing, thrill-seeking dude with a deep appreciation for quality fruits and vegetables. He loves hanging out with his pal Bobby and if you are ever looking for a fun time filled with adventure, definitely call the Par-Dawg!

DR. ARTURO SANTIAGO

Arturo is amicably divorced from Ronnie Anne and Bobby's mother Maria, and he is a physician who was previously living and working in Peru with Physicians on Missions, an organization that cares for children and provides vaccines and health care in clinics throughout the world. Like his daughter, Dr. Santiago is adventurous, funny, kindhearted, and charismatic. He and Ronnie Anne share a special bond despite the (previous) distance. And you can definitely see where Bobby gets his silliness from! Even Hector can't help but smile when Arturo joins in on the fun.

"O POSSUM, WHERE ART THOU?!"

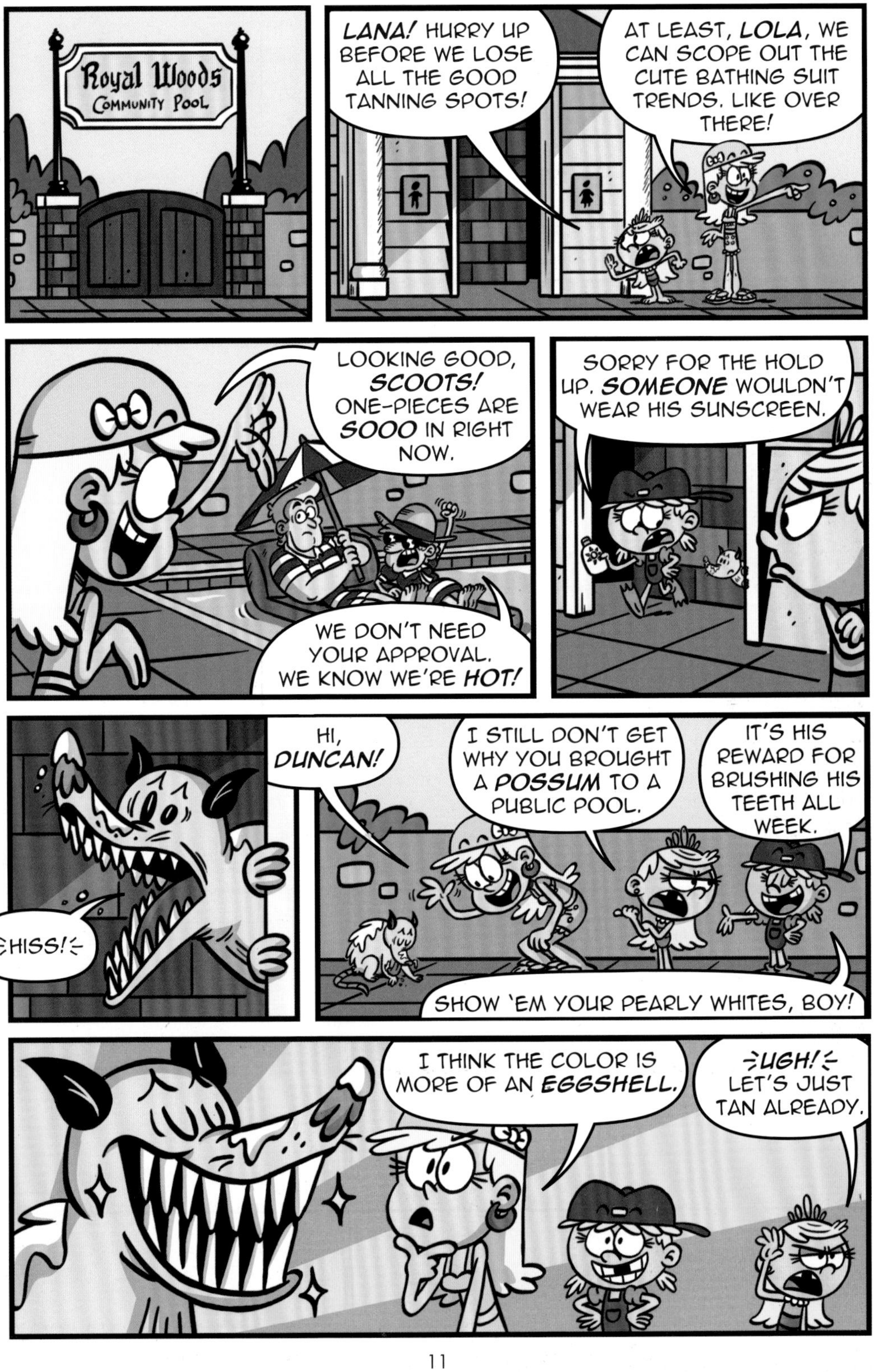
Royal Woods
Community Pool
LANA! HURRY UP BEFORE WE LOSE ALL THE GOOD TANNING SPOTS!
AT LEAST, LOLA, WE CAN SCOPE OUT THE CUTE BATHING SUIT TRENDS. LIKE OVER THERE!
LOOKING GOOD, SCOOTS! ONE-PIECES ARE SOOO IN RIGHT NOW.
WE DON'T NEED YOUR APPROVAL. WE KNOW WE'RE HOT!
SORRY FOR THE HOLD UP. SOMEONE WOULDN'T WEAR HIS SUNSCREEN.
HISS!
HI, DUNCAN!
I STILL DON'T GET WHY YOU BROUGHT A POSSUM TO A PUBLIC POOL.
IT'S HIS REWARD FOR BRUSHING HIS TEETH ALL WEEK.
SHOW 'EM YOUR PEARLY WHITES, BOY!
I THINK THE COLOR IS MORE OF AN EGGSHELL.
UGH! LET'S JUST TAN ALREADY.

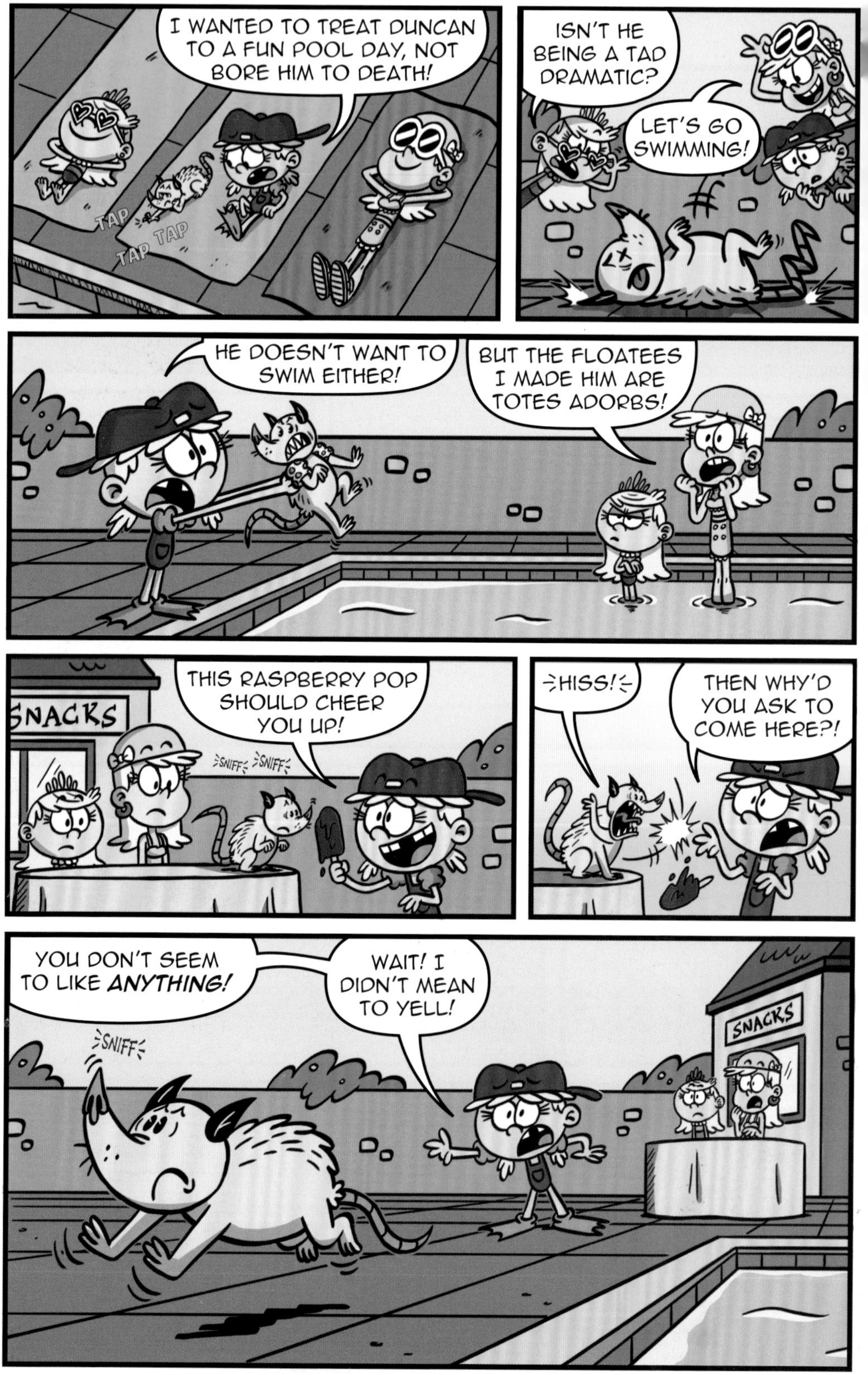
I WANTED TO TREAT DUNCAN TO A FUN POOL DAY, NOT BORE HIM TO DEATH!
TAP
TAP TAP
ISN'T HE BEING A TAD DRAMATIC?
LET'S GO SWIMMING!
HE DOESN'T WANT TO SWIM EITHER!
BUT THE FLOATEES I MADE HIM ARE TOTES ADORBS!
SNACKS
THIS RASPBERRY POP SHOULD CHEER YOU UP!
SNIFF SNIFF
HISS!
THEN WHY'D YOU ASK TO COME HERE?!
YOU DON'T SEEM TO LIKE ***ANYTHING!***
WAIT! I DIDN'T MEAN TO YELL!
SNIFF
SNACKS

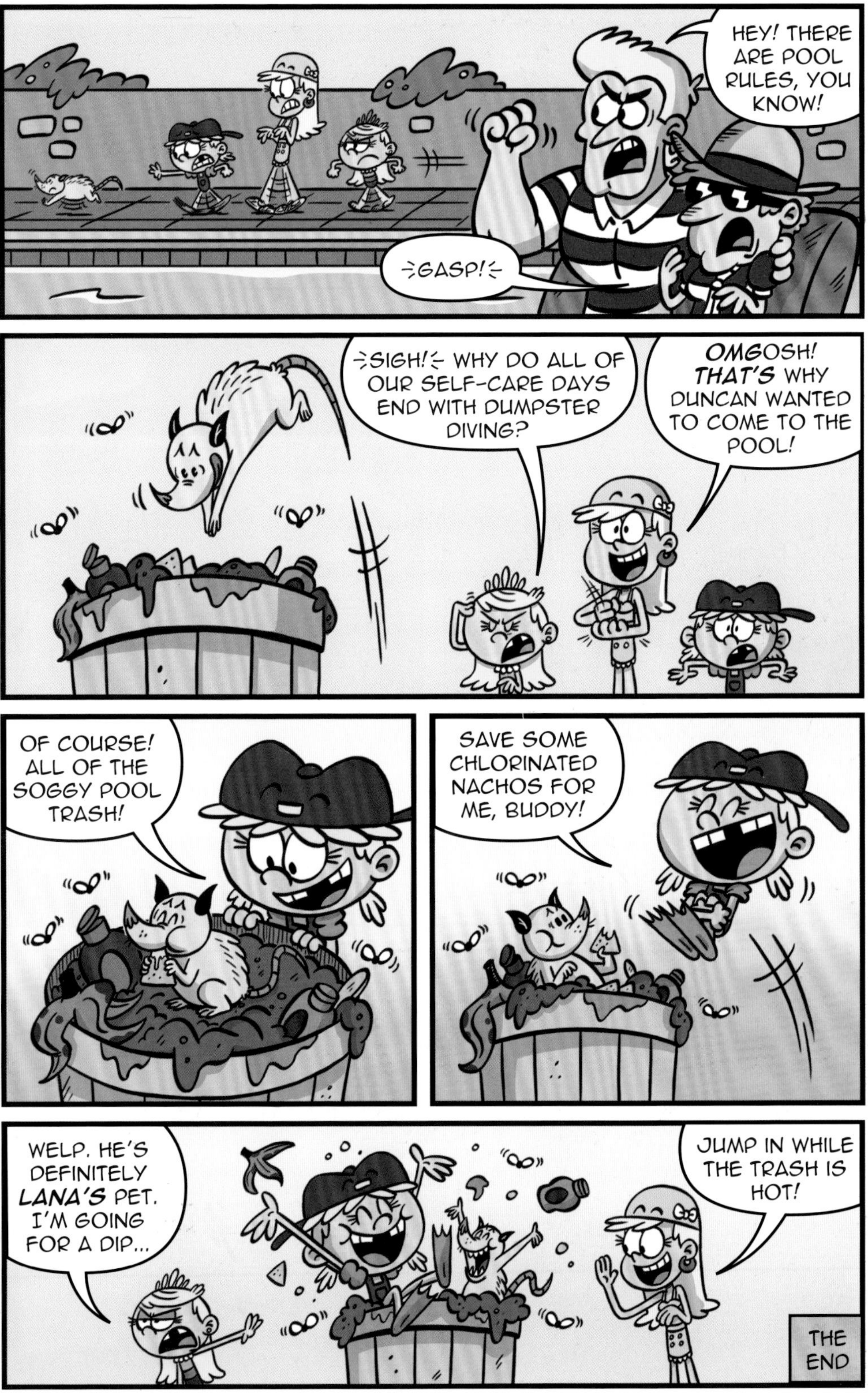
HEY! THERE ARE POOL RULES, YOU KNOW!
GASP!
SIGH! WHY DO ALL OF OUR SELF-CARE DAYS END WITH DUMPSTER DIVING?
OMGOSH! THAT'S WHY DUNCAN WANTED TO COME TO THE POOL!
OF COURSE! ALL OF THE SOGGY POOL TRASH!
SAVE SOME CHLORINATED NACHOS FOR ME, BUDDY!
WELP. HE'S DEFINITELY LANA'S PET. I'M GOING FOR A DIP...
JUMP IN WHILE THE TRASH IS HOT!
THE END

"BOBBY IN DISTRESS"

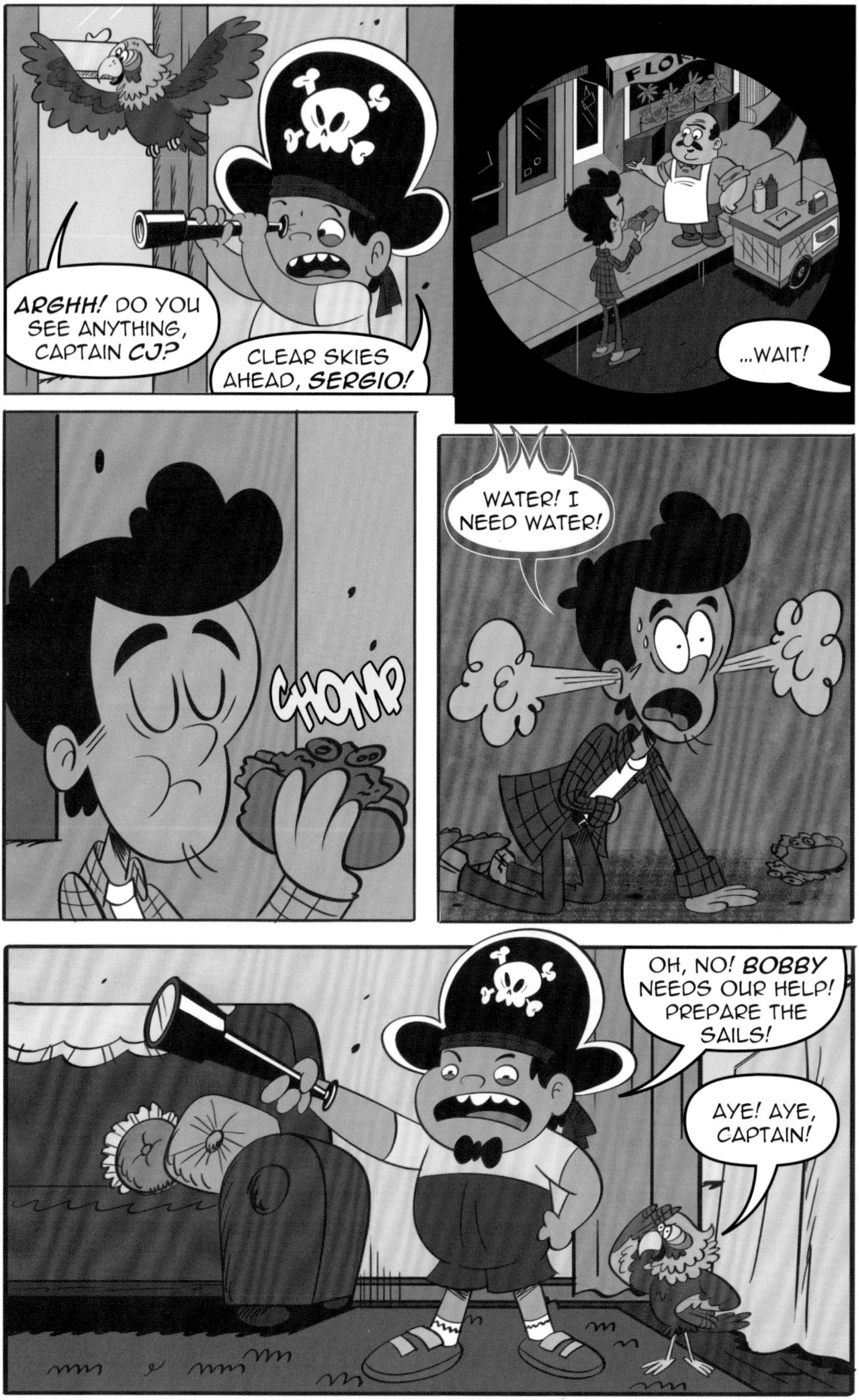

ARGHH! DO YOU SEE ANYTHING, CAPTAIN CJ?
CLEAR SKIES AHEAD, SERGIO!
...WAIT!
CHOMP
WATER! I NEED WATER!
OH, NO! BOBBY NEEDS OUR HELP! PREPARE THE SAILS!
AYE! AYE, CAPTAIN!

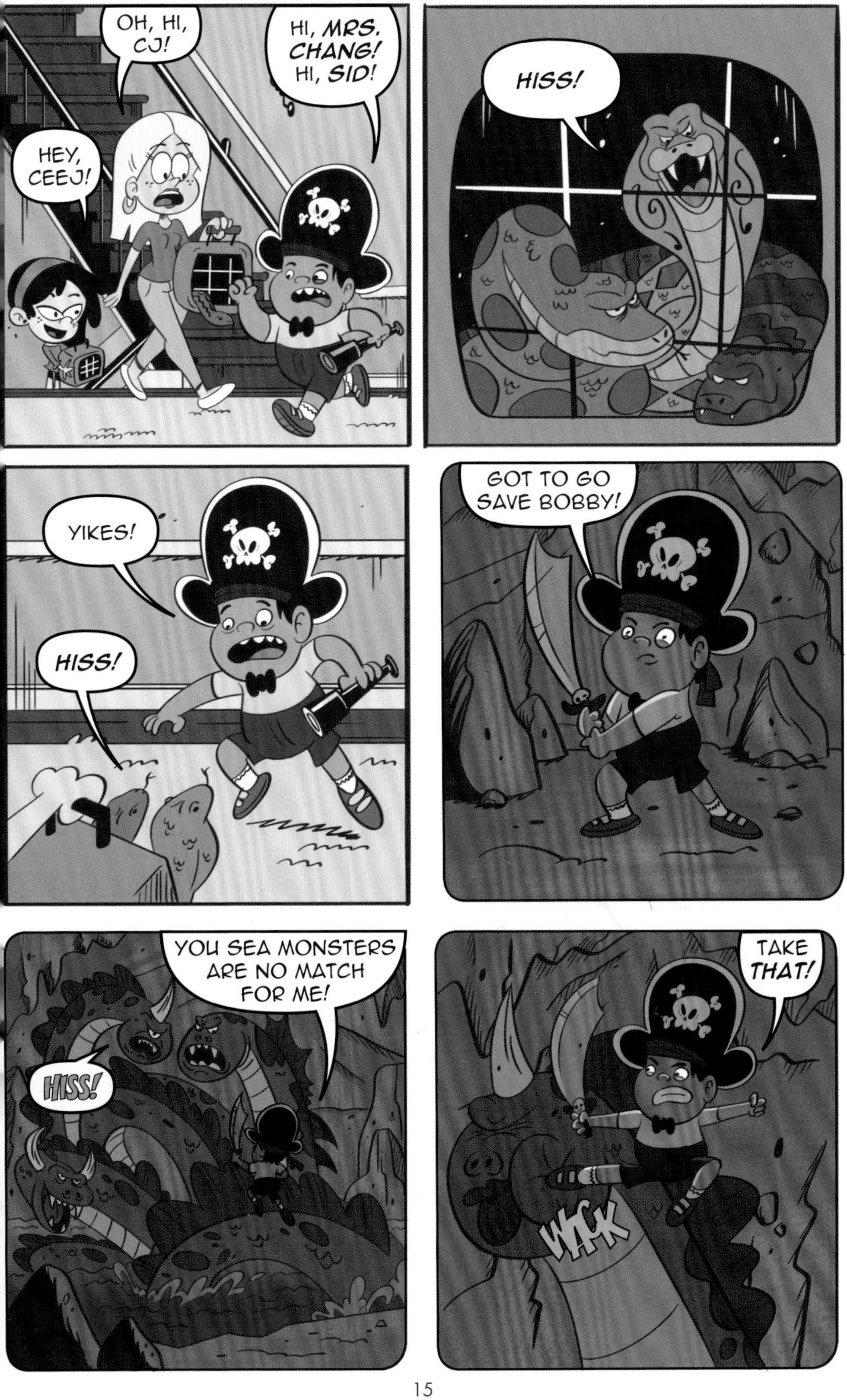
OH, HI, CJ!
HI, MRS. CHANG! HI, SID!
HEY, CEEJ!
HISS!
YIKES!
HISS!
GOT TO GO SAVE BOBBY!
YOU SEA MONSTERS ARE NO MATCH FOR ME!
HISS!
TAKE THAT!
WACK

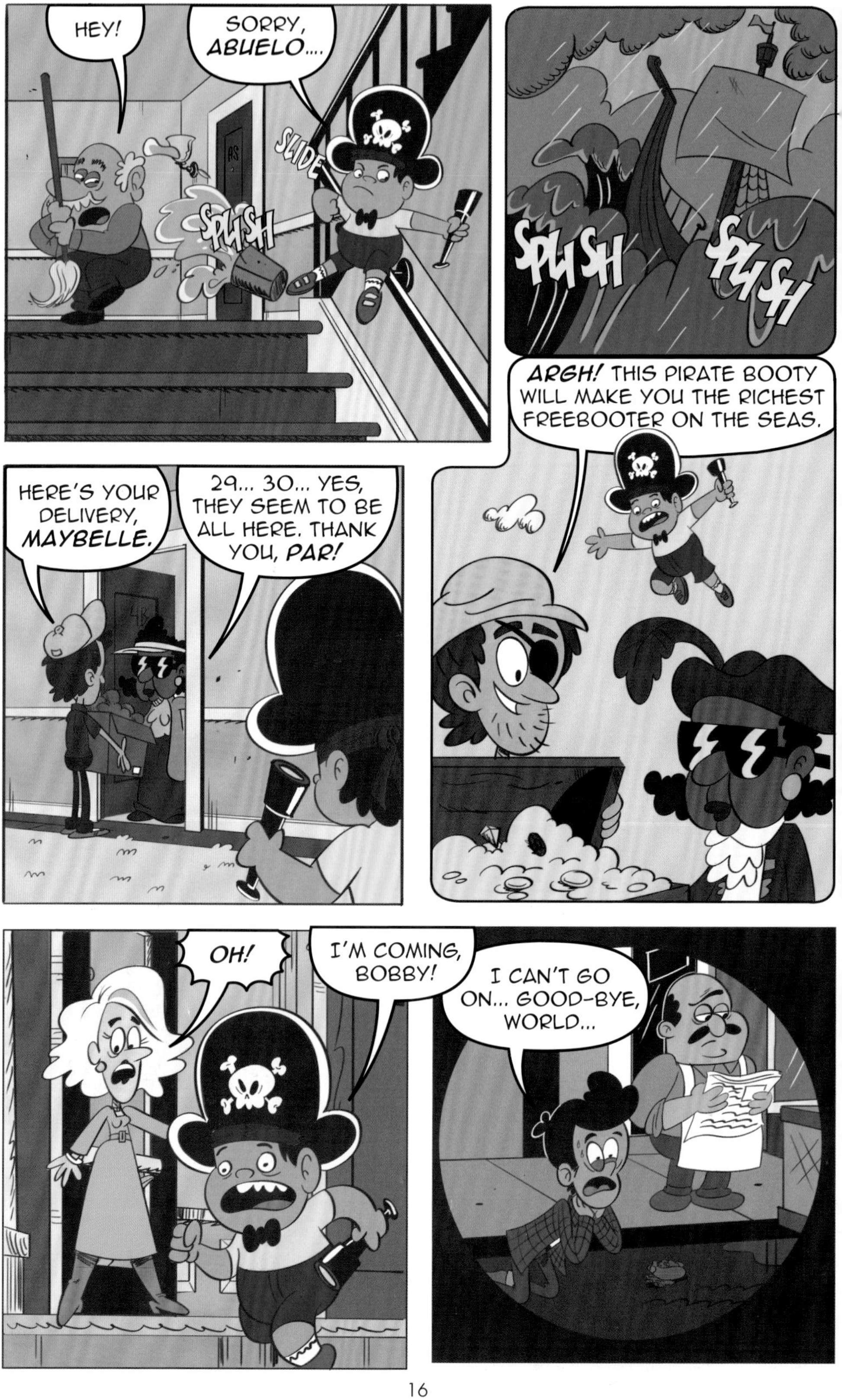
HEY!
SORRY, ABUELO....
SLIDE
SPLISH
SPLISH
SPLISH
ARGH! THIS PIRATE BOOTY WILL MAKE YOU THE RICHEST FREEBOOTER ON THE SEAS.
HERE'S YOUR DELIVERY, MAYBELLE.
29... 30... YES, THEY SEEM TO BE ALL HERE. THANK YOU, PAR!
OH!
I'M COMING, BOBBY!
I CAN'T GO ON... GOOD-BYE, WORLD...

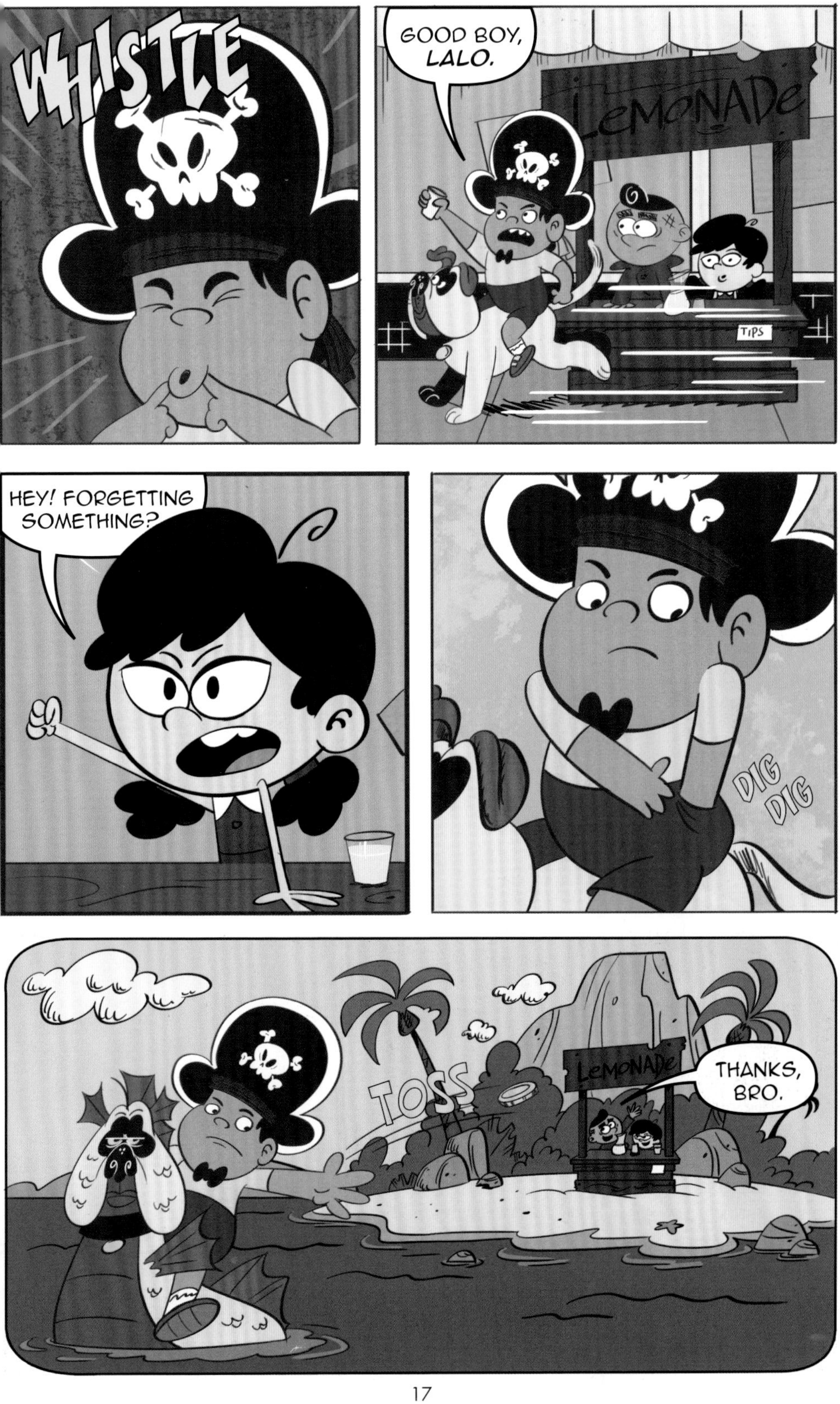
WHISTLE
GOOD BOY, LALO.
LEMONADE
TIPS
HEY! FORGETTING SOMETHING?
DIG DIG
TOSS
LEMONADE
THANKS, BRO.

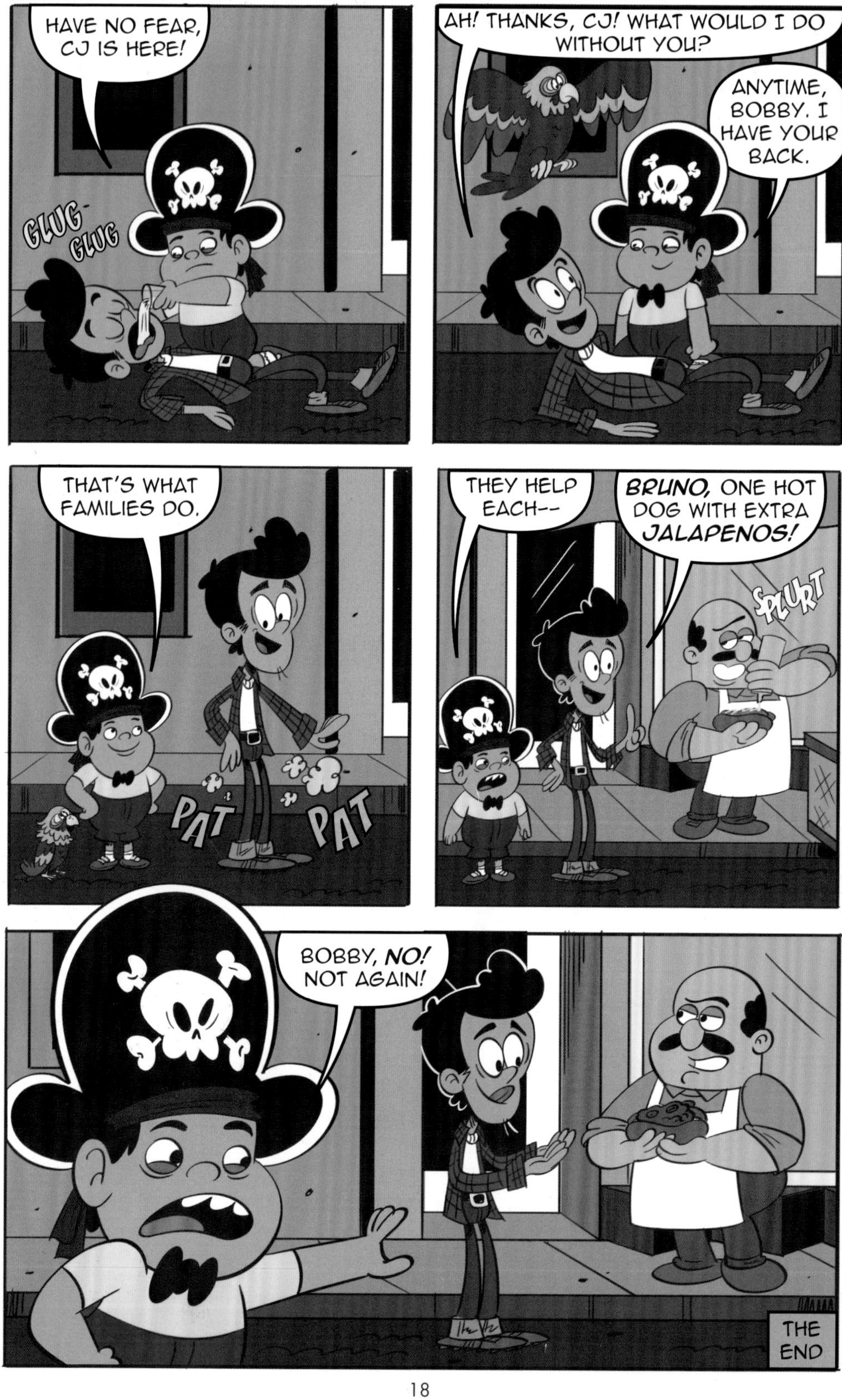
HAVE NO FEAR, CJ IS HERE!
GLUG-GLUG
AH! THANKS, CJ! WHAT WOULD I DO WITHOUT YOU?
ANYTIME, BOBBY. I HAVE YOUR BACK.
THAT'S WHAT FAMILIES DO.
PAT PAT
THEY HELP EACH--
BRUNO, ONE HOT DOG WITH EXTRA JALAPENOS!
SPLURT
BOBBY, NO! NOT AGAIN!
THE END

"WE WILL ROCK YOU"

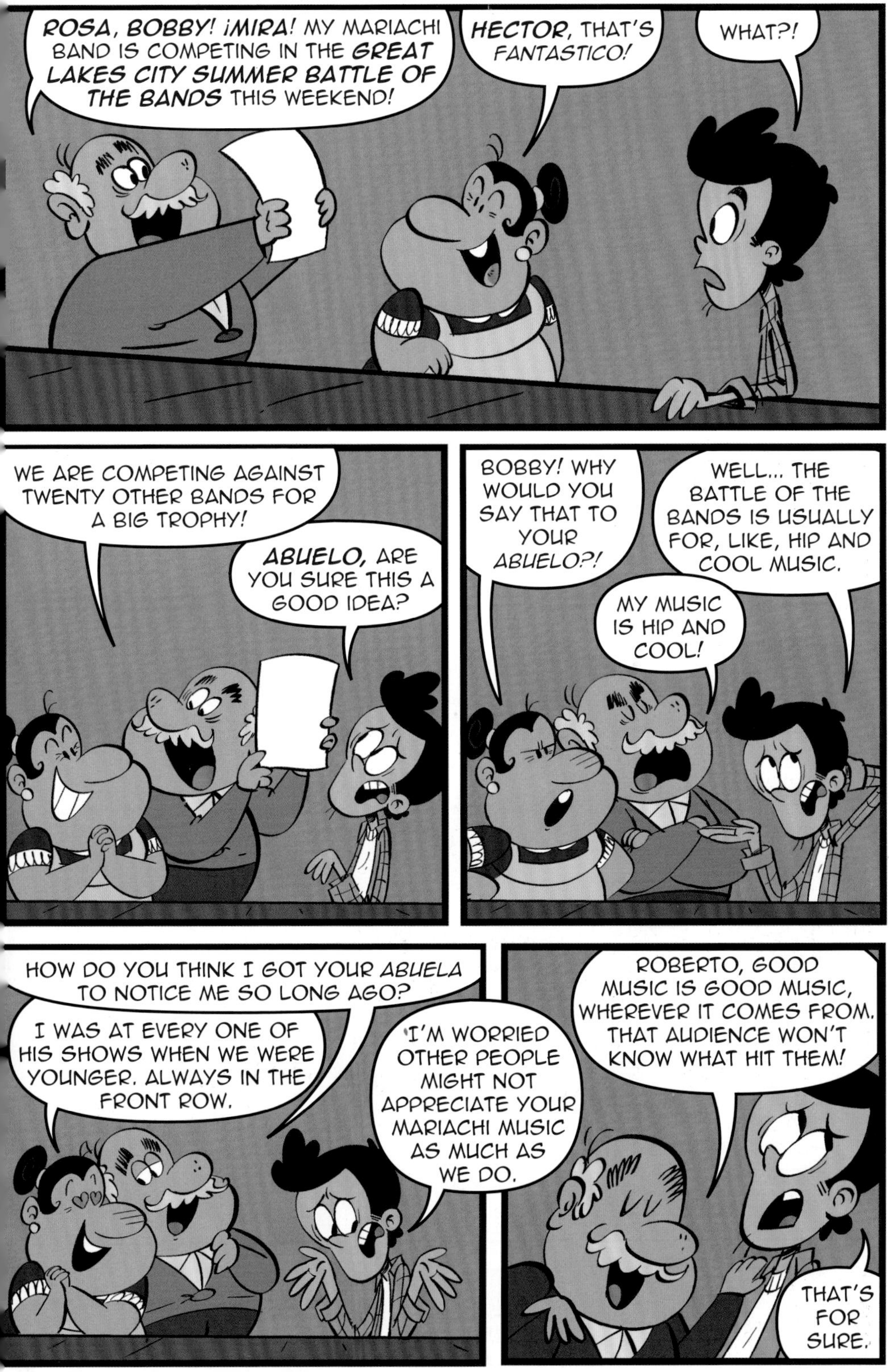
ROSA, BOBBY! ¡MIRA! MY MARIACHI BAND IS COMPETING IN THE GREAT LAKES CITY SUMMER BATTLE OF THE BANDS THIS WEEKEND!
HECTOR, THAT'S FANTASTICO!
WHAT?!
WE ARE COMPETING AGAINST TWENTY OTHER BANDS FOR A BIG TROPHY!
ABUELO, ARE YOU SURE THIS A GOOD IDEA?
BOBBY! WHY WOULD YOU SAY THAT TO YOUR ABUELO?!
WELL... THE BATTLE OF THE BANDS IS USUALLY FOR, LIKE, HIP AND COOL MUSIC.
MY MUSIC IS HIP AND COOL!
HOW DO YOU THINK I GOT YOUR ABUELA TO NOTICE ME SO LONG AGO?
I WAS AT EVERY ONE OF HIS SHOWS WHEN WE WERE YOUNGER. ALWAYS IN THE FRONT ROW.
I'M WORRIED OTHER PEOPLE MIGHT NOT APPRECIATE YOUR MARIACHI MUSIC AS MUCH AS WE DO.
ROBERTO, GOOD MUSIC IS GOOD MUSIC, WHEREVER IT COMES FROM. THAT AUDIENCE WON'T KNOW WHAT HIT THEM!
THAT'S FOR SURE.

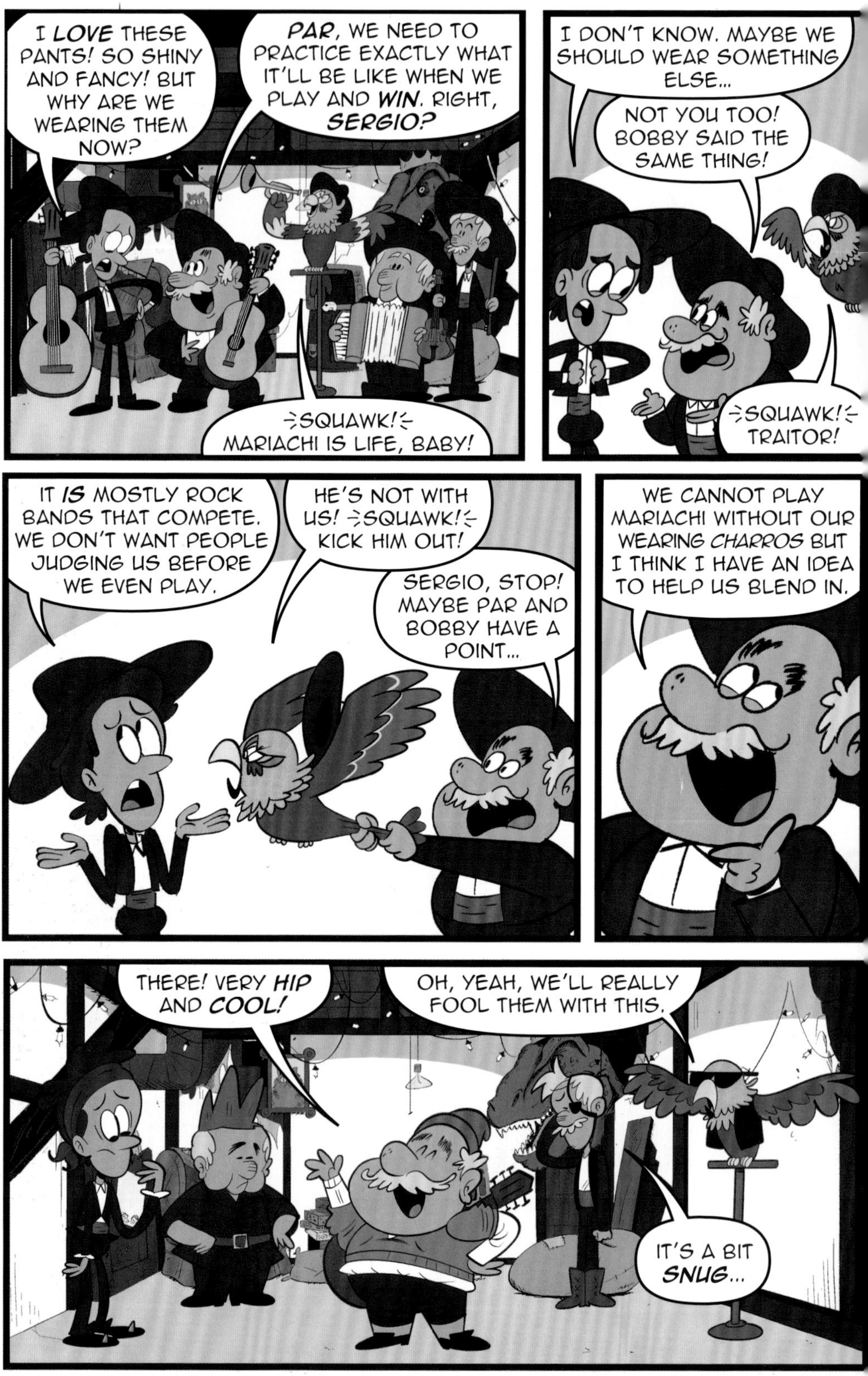

I LOVE THESE PANTS! SO SHINY AND FANCY! BUT WHY ARE WE WEARING THEM NOW?
PAR, WE NEED TO PRACTICE EXACTLY WHAT IT'LL BE LIKE WHEN WE PLAY AND WIN. RIGHT, SERGIO?
SQUAWK! MARIACHI IS LIFE, BABY!
I DON'T KNOW. MAYBE WE SHOULD WEAR SOMETHING ELSE...
NOT YOU TOO! BOBBY SAID THE SAME THING!
SQUAWK! TRAITOR!
IT IS MOSTLY ROCK BANDS THAT COMPETE. WE DON'T WANT PEOPLE JUDGING US BEFORE WE EVEN PLAY.
HE'S NOT WITH US! SQUAWK! KICK HIM OUT!
SERGIO, STOP! MAYBE PAR AND BOBBY HAVE A POINT...
WE CANNOT PLAY MARIACHI WITHOUT OUR WEARING CHARROS BUT I THINK I HAVE AN IDEA TO HELP US BLEND IN.
THERE! VERY HIP AND COOL!
OH, YEAH, WE'LL REALLY FOOL THEM WITH THIS.
IT'S A BIT SNUG...

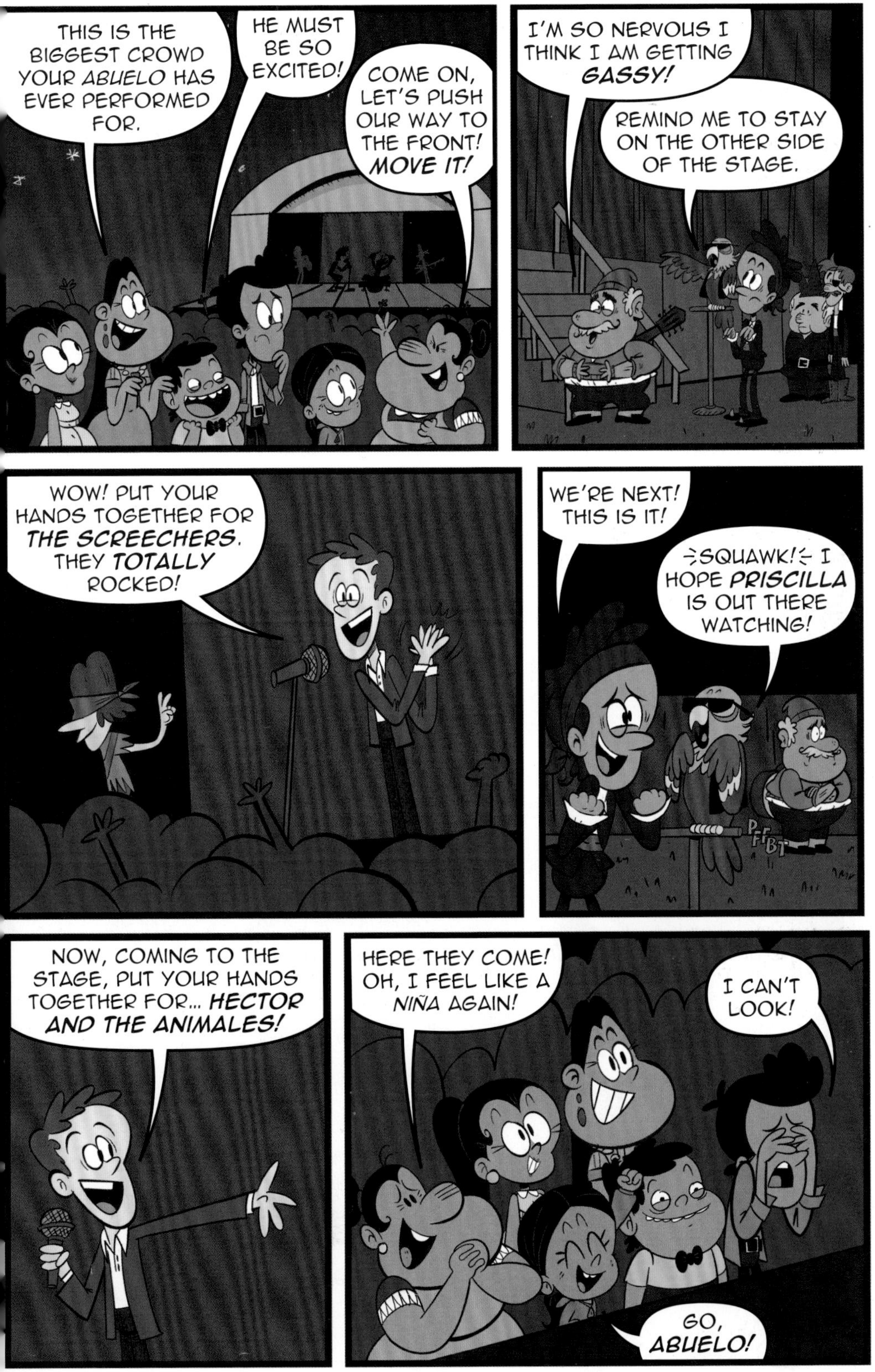
THIS IS THE BIGGEST CROWD YOUR ABUELO HAS EVER PERFORMED FOR.
HE MUST BE SO EXCITED!
COME ON, LET'S PUSH OUR WAY TO THE FRONT! MOVE IT!
I'M SO NERVOUS I THINK I AM GETTING GASSY!
REMIND ME TO STAY ON THE OTHER SIDE OF THE STAGE.
WOW! PUT YOUR HANDS TOGETHER FOR THE SCREECHERS. THEY TOTALLY ROCKED!
WE'RE NEXT! THIS IS IT!
SQUAWK! I HOPE PRISCILLA IS OUT THERE WATCHING!
PFFBT
NOW, COMING TO THE STAGE, PUT YOUR HANDS TOGETHER FOR... HECTOR AND THE ANIMALES!
HERE THEY COME! OH, I FEEL LIKE A NIÑA AGAIN!
I CAN'T LOOK!
GO, ABUELO!

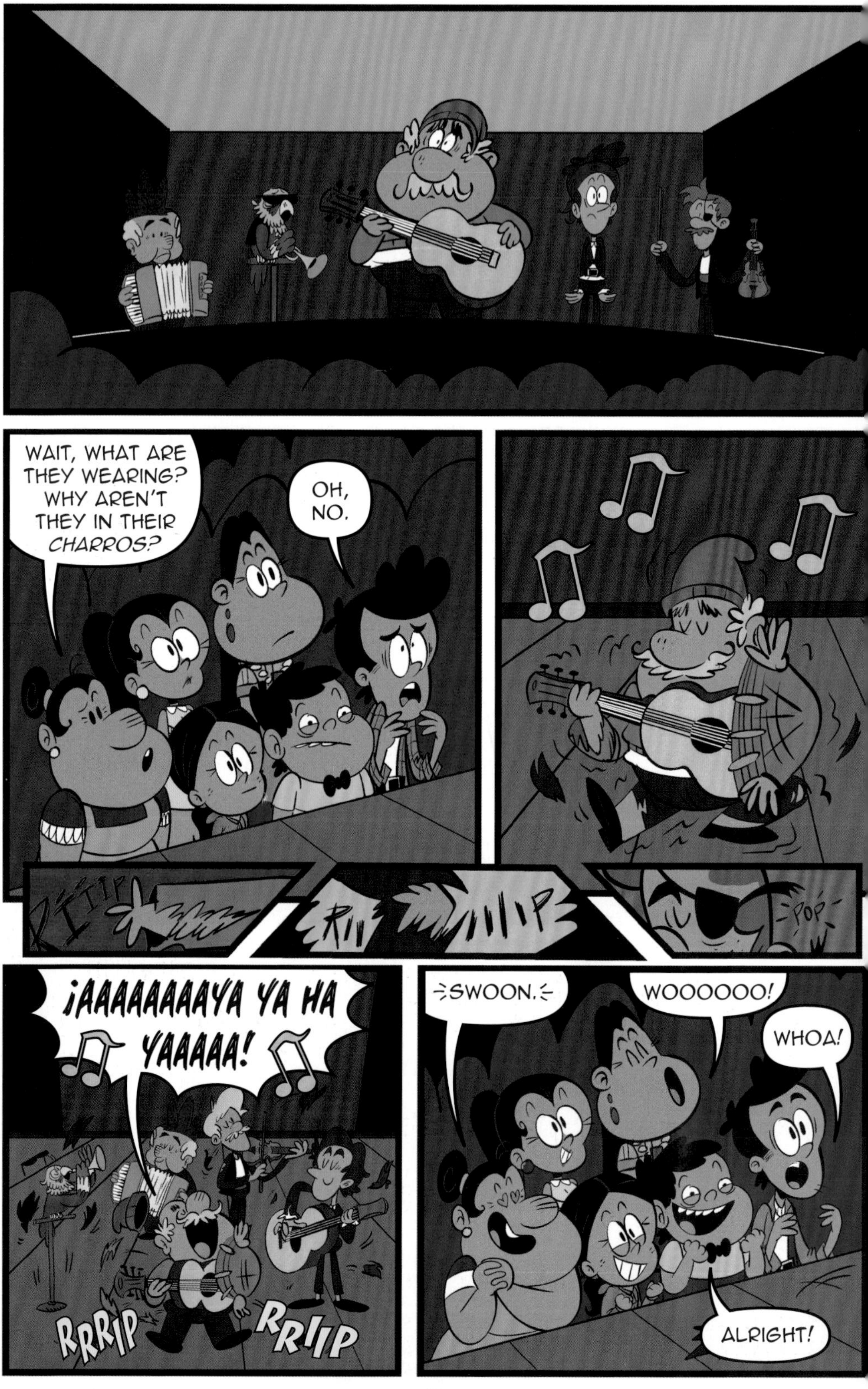
WAIT, WHAT ARE THEY WEARING? WHY AREN'T THEY IN THEIR CHARROS?
OH, NO.
RIIIP
RIIIIP
POP
¡AAAAAAAAYA YA HA YAAAAA!
RRRIP
RRIIP
SWOON.
WOOOOOO!
WHOA!
ALRIGHT!

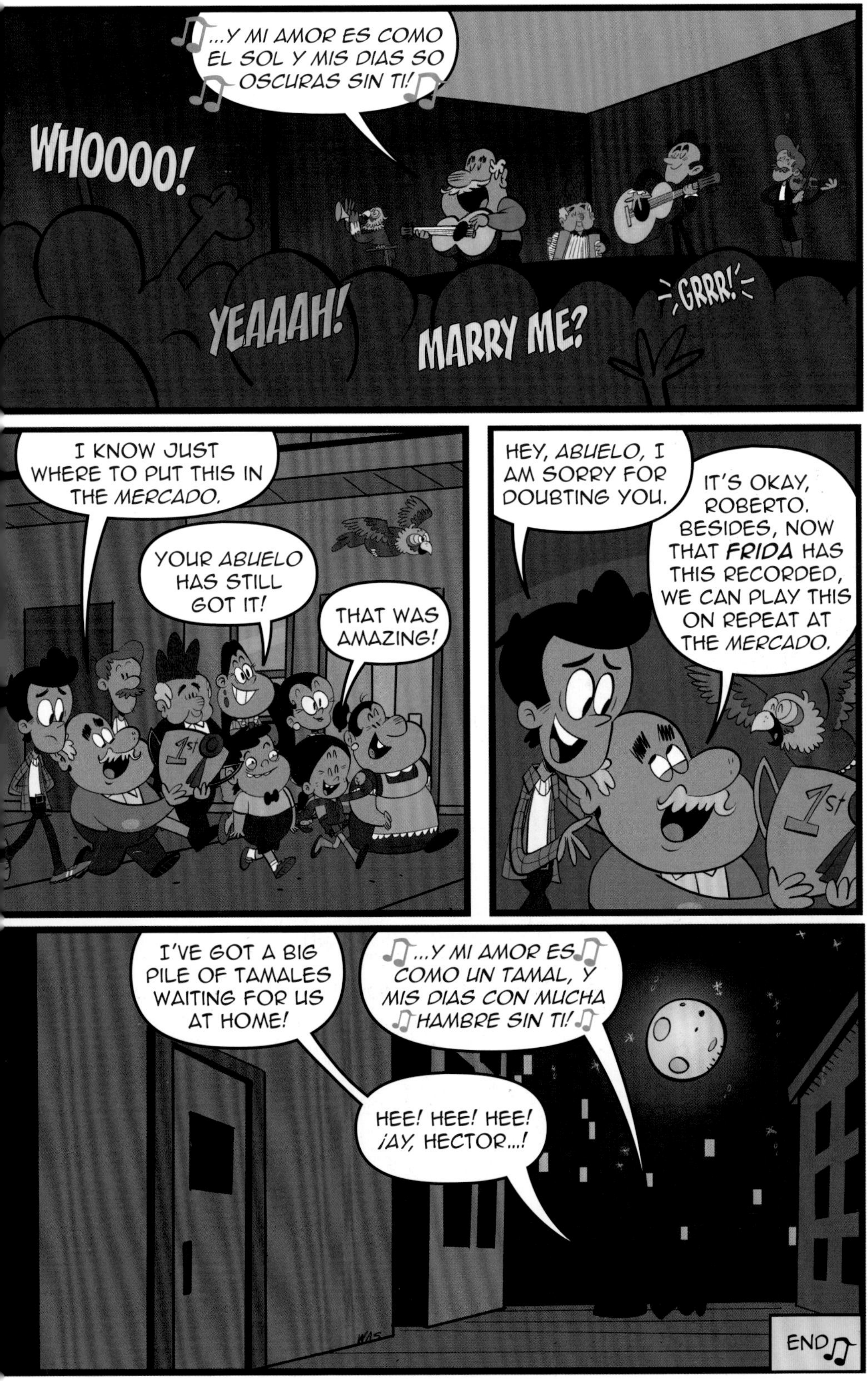
...Y MI AMOR ES COMO EL SOL Y MIS DIAS SO OSCURAS SIN TI!
WHOOOO!
YEAAAH!
MARRY ME?
GRRR!
I KNOW JUST WHERE TO PUT THIS IN THE MERCADO.
YOUR ABUELO HAS STILL GOT IT!
THAT WAS AMAZING!
HEY, ABUELO, I AM SORRY FOR DOUBTING YOU.
IT'S OKAY, ROBERTO. BESIDES, NOW THAT FRIDA HAS THIS RECORDED, WE CAN PLAY THIS ON REPEAT AT THE MERCADO.
I'VE GOT A BIG PILE OF TAMALES WAITING FOR US AT HOME!
...Y MI AMOR ES COMO UN TAMAL, Y MIS DIAS CON MUCHA HAMBRE SIN TI!
HEE! HEE! HEE! ¡AY, HECTOR...!
END

"WHAT GOES UP..."

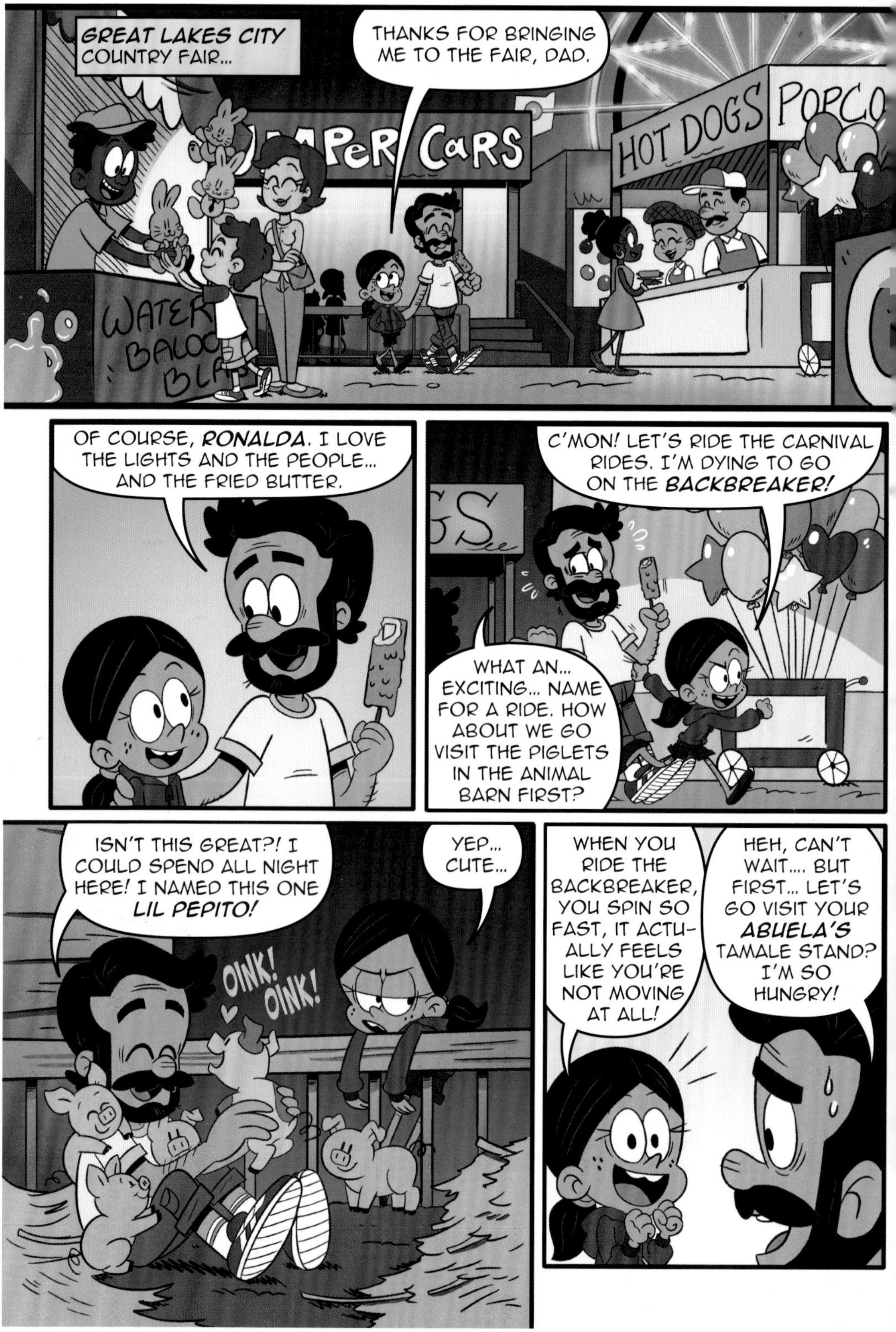
GREAT LAKES CITY COUNTRY FAIR...
THANKS FOR BRINGING ME TO THE FAIR, DAD.
HOT DOGS
OF COURSE, RONALDA. I LOVE THE LIGHTS AND THE PEOPLE... AND THE FRIED BUTTER.
C'MON! LET'S RIDE THE CARNIVAL RIDES. I'M DYING TO GO ON THE BACKBREAKER!
WHAT AN... EXCITING... NAME FOR A RIDE. HOW ABOUT WE GO VISIT THE PIGLETS IN THE ANIMAL BARN FIRST?
ISN'T THIS GREAT?! I COULD SPEND ALL NIGHT HERE! I NAMED THIS ONE LIL PEPITO!
OINK! OINK!
YEP... CUTE...
WHEN YOU RIDE THE BACKBREAKER, YOU SPIN SO FAST, IT ACTUALLY FEELS LIKE YOU'RE NOT MOVING AT ALL!
HEH, CAN'T WAIT.... BUT FIRST... LET'S GO VISIT YOUR ABUELA'S TAMALE STAND? I'M SO HUNGRY!

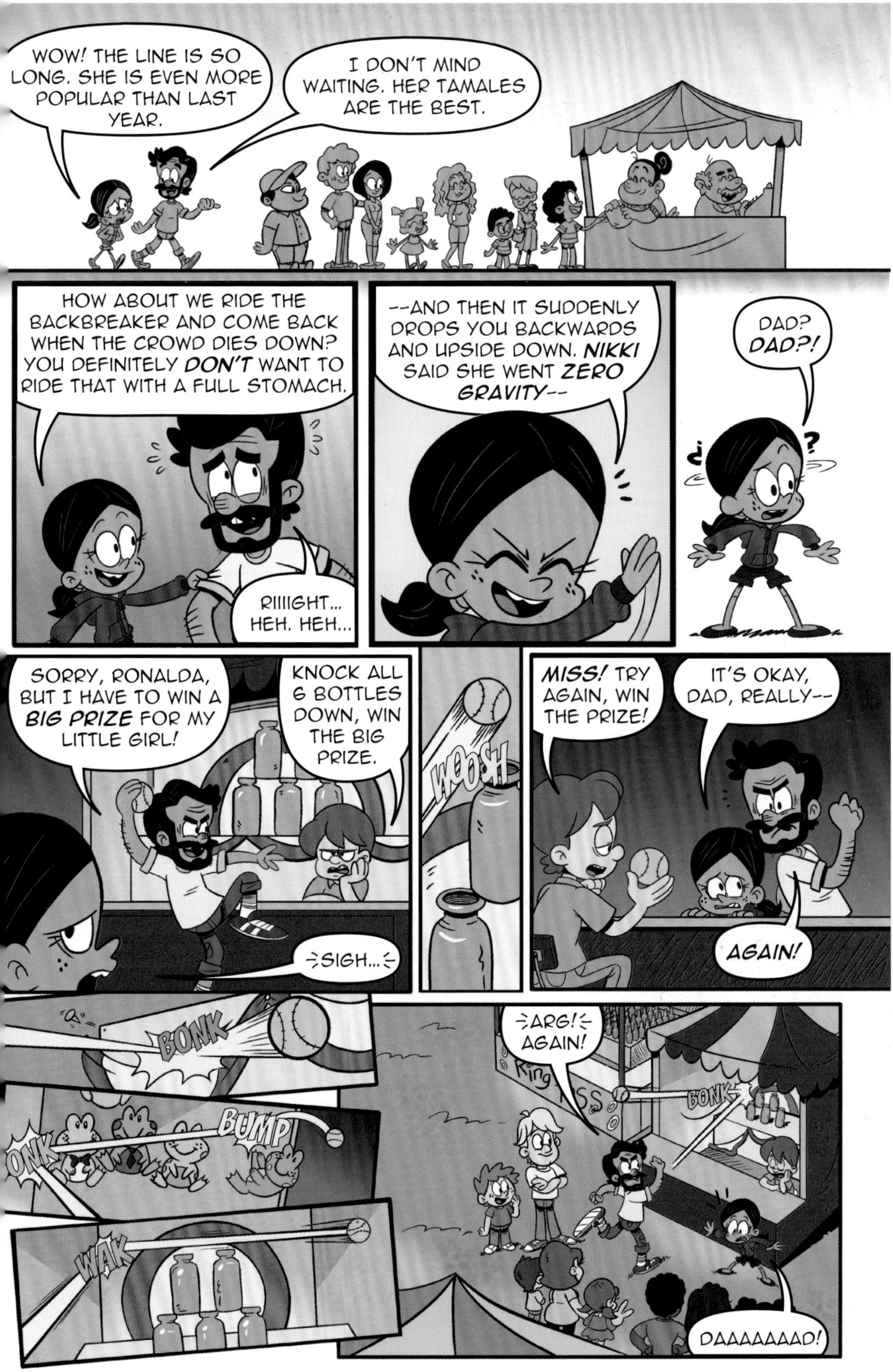
WOW! THE LINE IS SO LONG. SHE IS EVEN MORE POPULAR THAN LAST YEAR.
I DON'T MIND WAITING. HER TAMALES ARE THE BEST.
HOW ABOUT WE RIDE THE BACKBREAKER AND COME BACK WHEN THE CROWD DIES DOWN? YOU DEFINITELY DON'T WANT TO RIDE THAT WITH A FULL STOMACH.
RIIIIGHT... HEH. HEH...
--AND THEN IT SUDDENLY DROPS YOU BACKWARDS AND UPSIDE DOWN. NIKKI SAID SHE WENT ZERO GRAVITY--
DAD? DAD?!
SORRY, RONALDA, BUT I HAVE TO WIN A BIG PRIZE FOR MY LITTLE GIRL!
KNOCK ALL 6 BOTTLES DOWN, WIN THE BIG PRIZE.
SIGH...
WOOSH
MISS! TRY AGAIN, WIN THE PRIZE!
IT'S OKAY, DAD, REALLY--
AGAIN!
BONK
BUMP
ONK
WAK
ARG! AGAIN!
BONK
DAAAAAAAD!

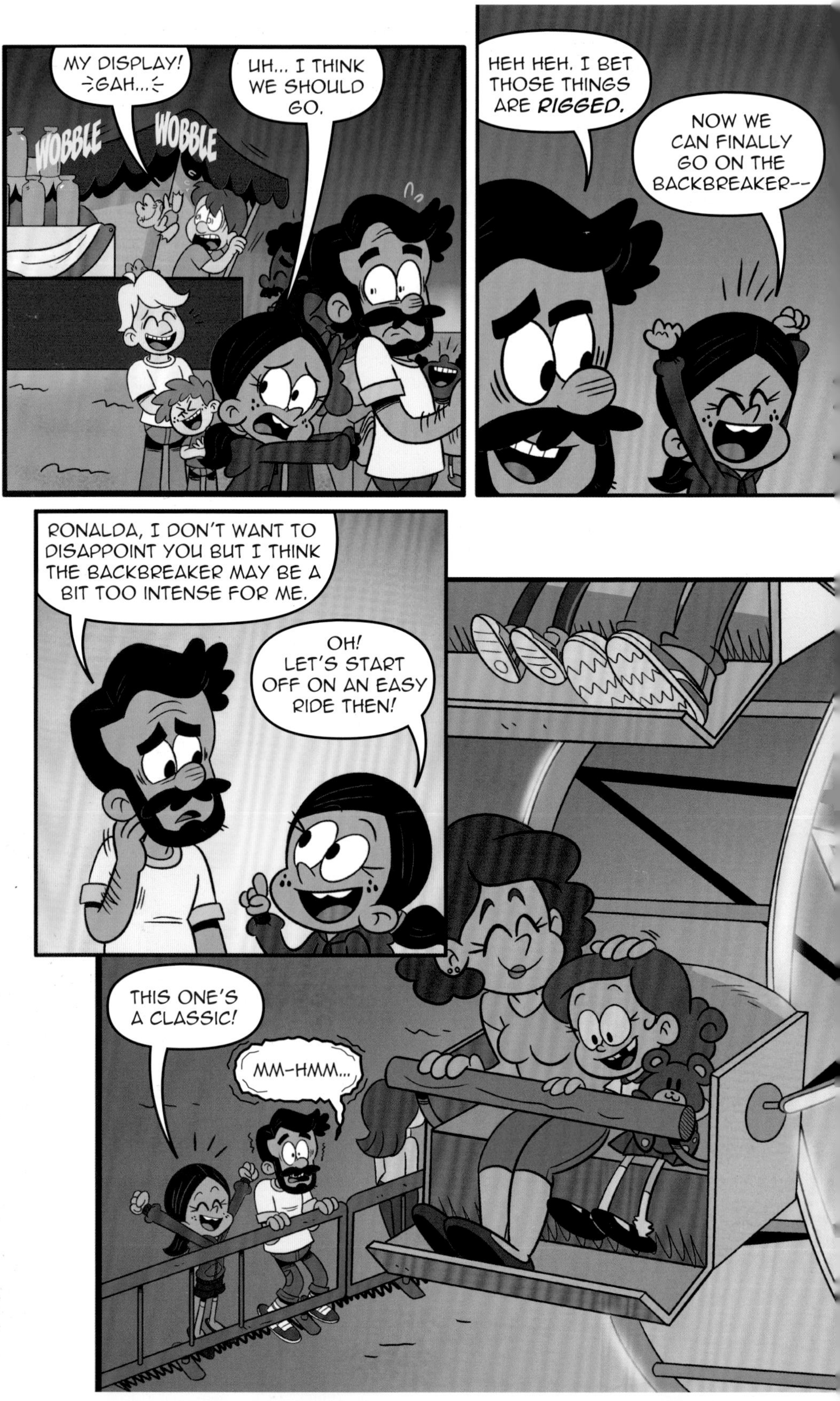
MY DISPLAY! GAH...
WOBBLE
WOBBLE
UH... I THINK WE SHOULD GO.
HEH HEH. I BET THOSE THINGS ARE *RIGGED.*
NOW WE CAN FINALLY GO ON THE BACKBREAKER--
RONALDA, I DON'T WANT TO DISAPPOINT YOU BUT I THINK THE BACKBREAKER MAY BE A BIT TOO INTENSE FOR ME.
OH! LET'S START OFF ON AN EASY RIDE THEN!
THIS ONE'S A CLASSIC!
MM-HMM...

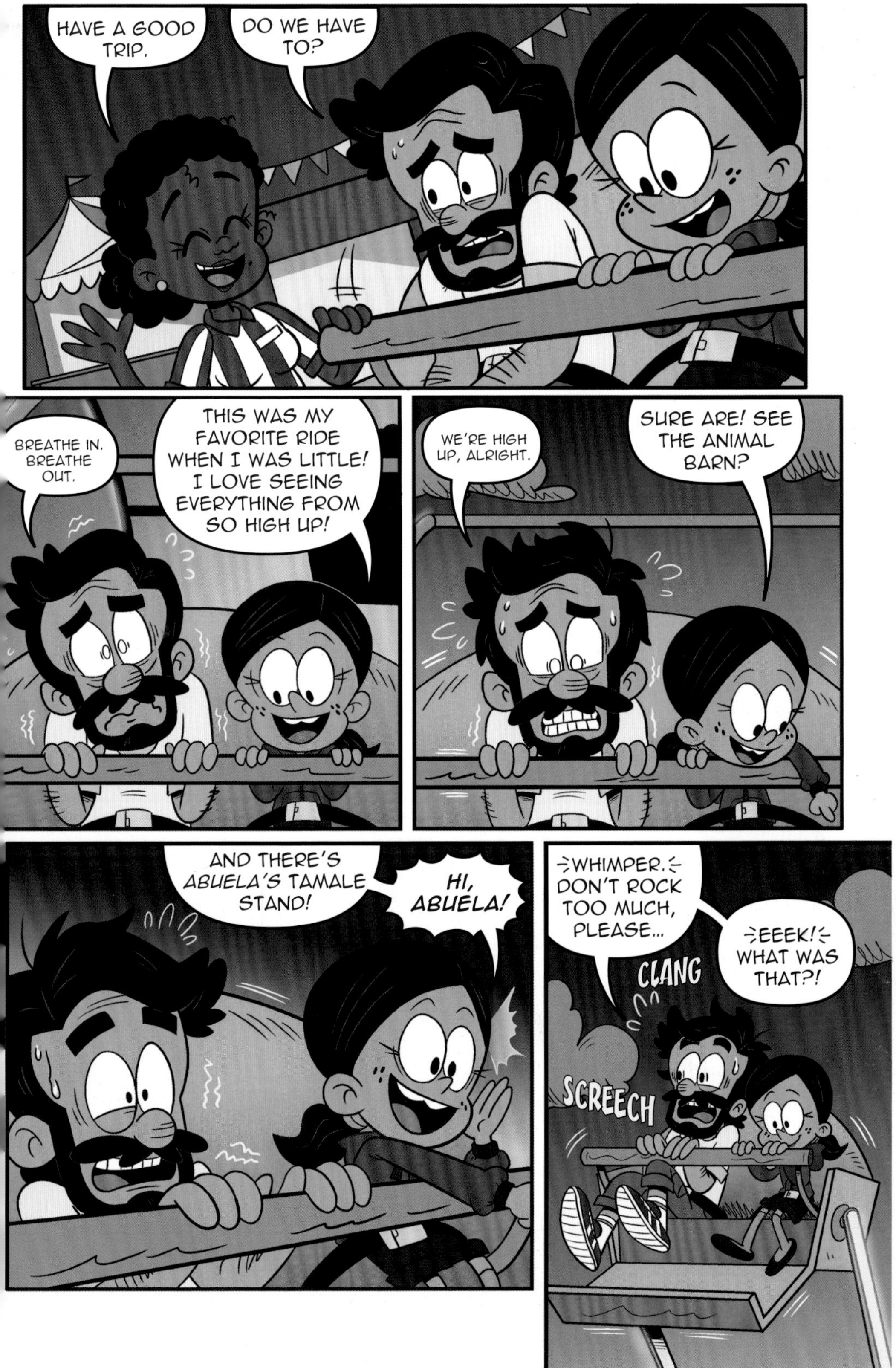

HAVE A GOOD TRIP.
DO WE HAVE TO?
BREATHE IN. BREATHE OUT.
THIS WAS MY FAVORITE RIDE WHEN I WAS LITTLE! I LOVE SEEING EVERYTHING FROM SO HIGH UP!
WE'RE HIGH UP, ALRIGHT.
SURE ARE! SEE THE ANIMAL BARN?
AND THERE'S ABUELA'S TAMALE STAND!
HI, ABUELA!
WHIMPER. DON'T ROCK TOO MUCH, PLEASE...
CLANG
SCREECH
EEEK! WHAT WAS THAT?!

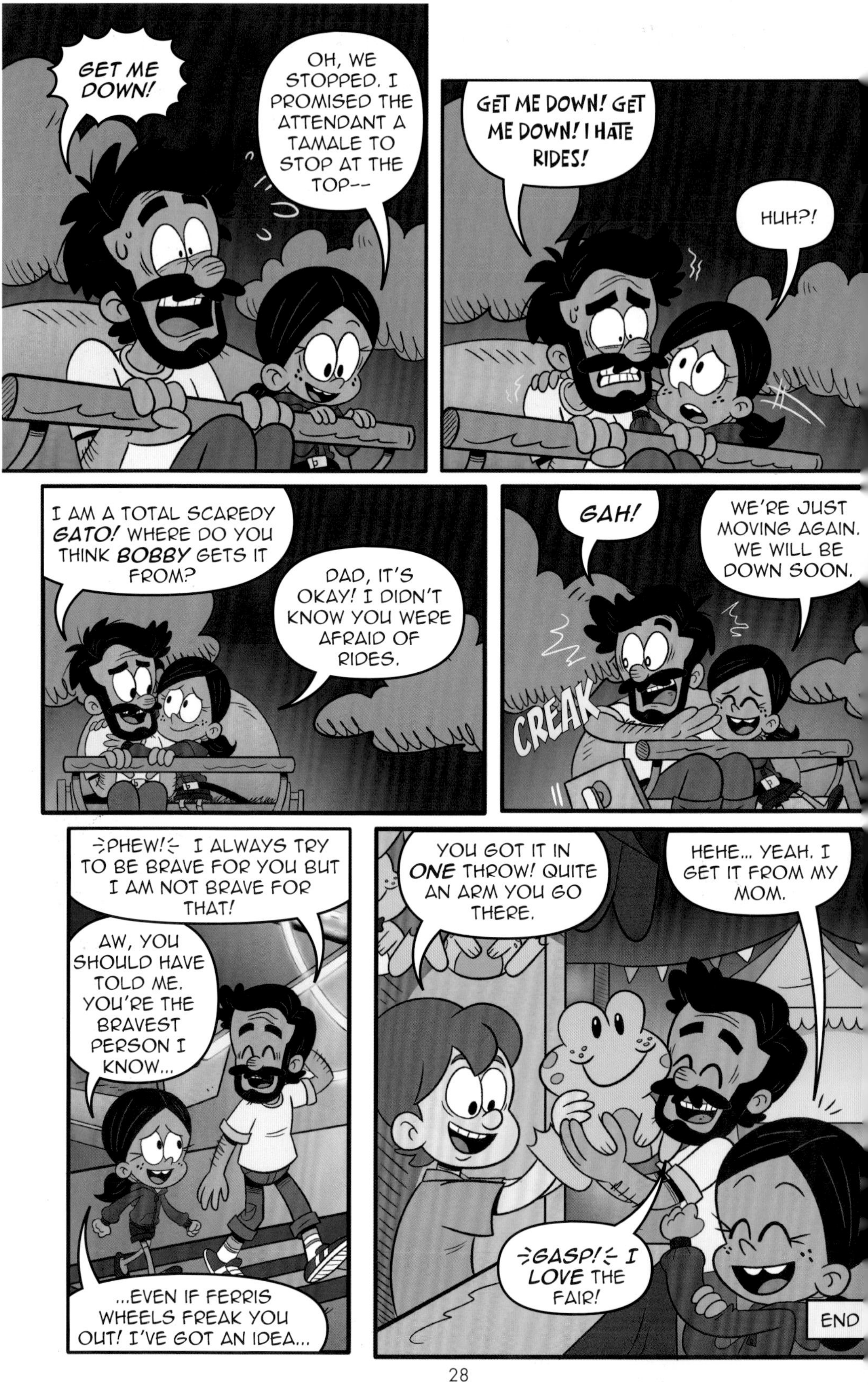
GET ME DOWN!
OH, WE STOPPED. I PROMISED THE ATTENDANT A TAMALE TO STOP AT THE TOP--
GET ME DOWN! GET ME DOWN! I HATE RIDES!
HUH?!
I AM A TOTAL SCAREDY GATO! WHERE DO YOU THINK BOBBY GETS IT FROM?
DAD, IT'S OKAY! I DIDN'T KNOW YOU WERE AFRAID OF RIDES.
GAH!
WE'RE JUST MOVING AGAIN. WE WILL BE DOWN SOON.
CREAK
PHEW! I ALWAYS TRY TO BE BRAVE FOR YOU BUT I AM NOT BRAVE FOR THAT!
AW, YOU SHOULD HAVE TOLD ME. YOU'RE THE BRAVEST PERSON I KNOW...
...EVEN IF FERRIS WHEELS FREAK YOU OUT! I'VE GOT AN IDEA...
YOU GOT IT IN ONE THROW! QUITE AN ARM YOU GO THERE.
HEHE... YEAH. I GET IT FROM MY MOM.
GASP! I LOVE THE FAIR!
END

"LUCY'S SUMMER FASHION TIPS"

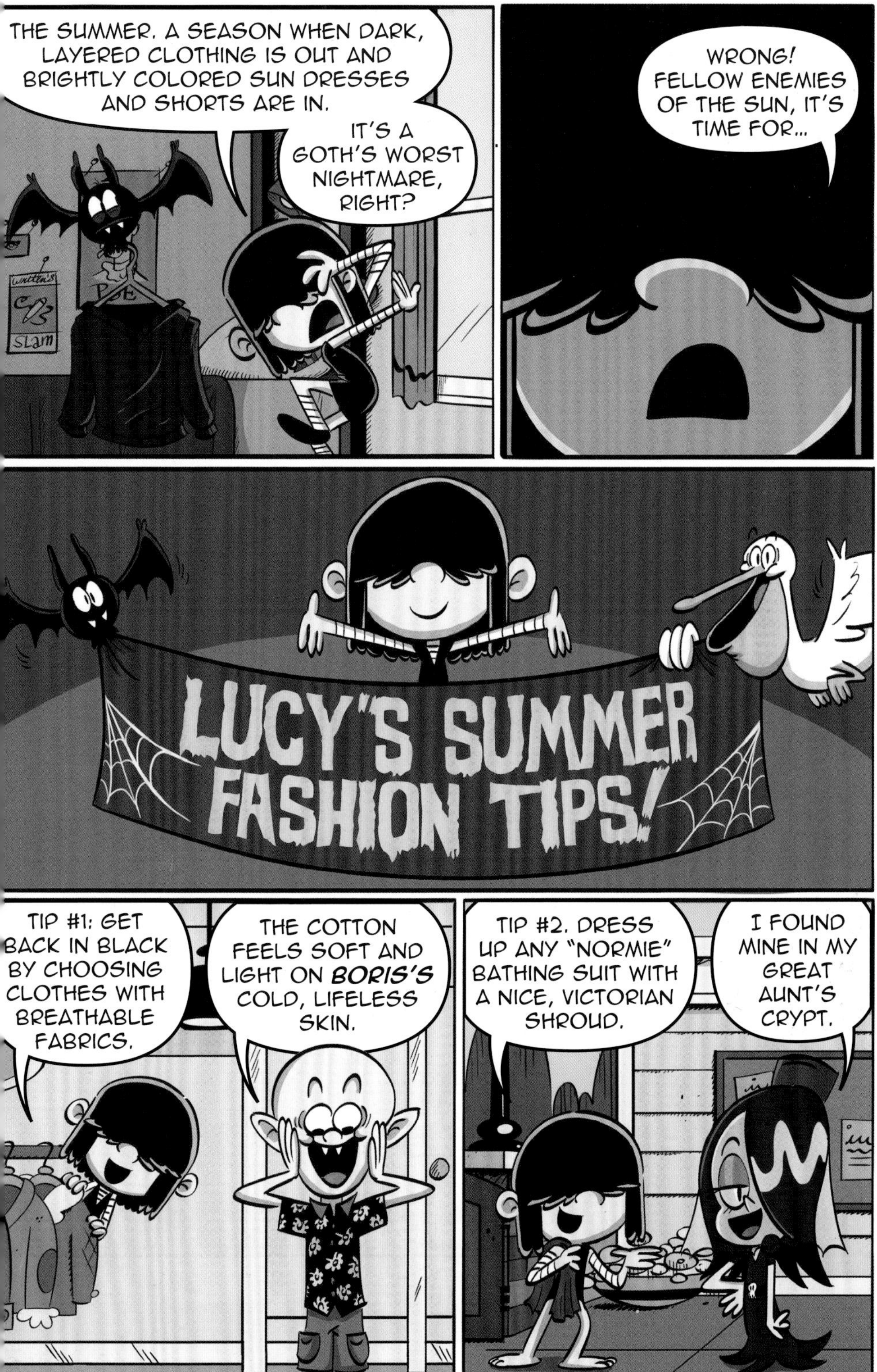

THE SUMMER. A SEASON WHEN DARK, LAYERED CLOTHING IS OUT AND BRIGHTLY COLORED SUN DRESSES AND SHORTS ARE IN.
IT'S A GOTH'S WORST NIGHTMARE, RIGHT?
written's
SLAM
WRONG! FELLOW ENEMIES OF THE SUN, IT'S TIME FOR...
LUCY'S SUMMER FASHION TIPS!
TIP #1: GET BACK IN BLACK BY CHOOSING CLOTHES WITH BREATHABLE FABRICS.
THE COTTON FEELS SOFT AND LIGHT ON ***BORIS'S*** COLD, LIFELESS SKIN.
TIP #2. DRESS UP ANY "NORMIE" BATHING SUIT WITH A NICE, VICTORIAN SHROUD.
I FOUND MINE IN MY GREAT AUNT'S CRYPT.

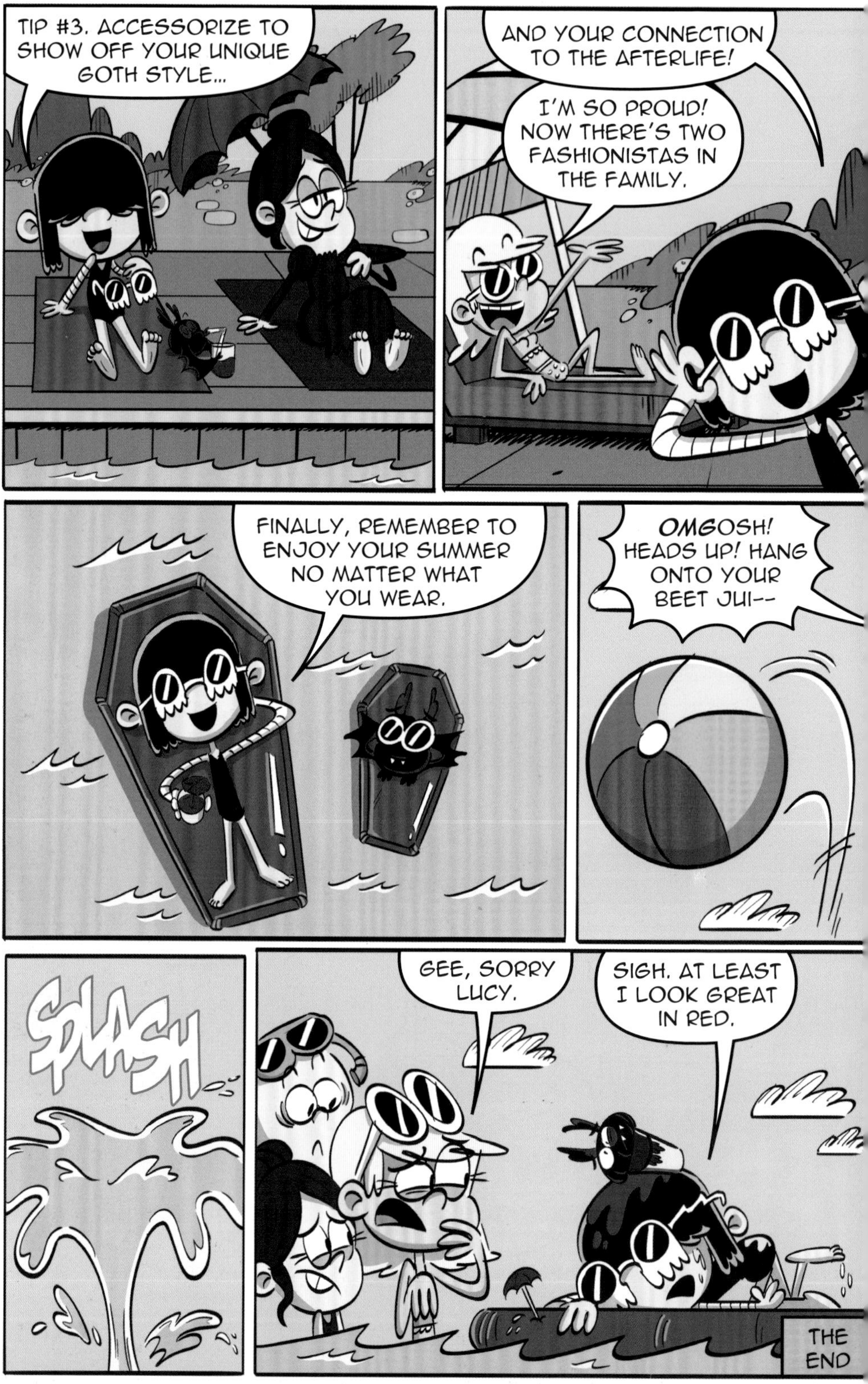
TIP #3. ACCESSORIZE TO SHOW OFF YOUR UNIQUE GOTH STYLE...
AND YOUR CONNECTION TO THE AFTERLIFE!
I'M SO PROUD! NOW THERE'S TWO FASHIONISTAS IN THE FAMILY.
FINALLY, REMEMBER TO ENJOY YOUR SUMMER NO MATTER WHAT YOU WEAR.
OMGOSH! HEADS UP! HANG ONTO YOUR BEET JUI--
SPLASH
GEE, SORRY LUCY.
SIGH. AT LEAST I LOOK GREAT IN RED.
THE END

"DOOM AND BLOOM"

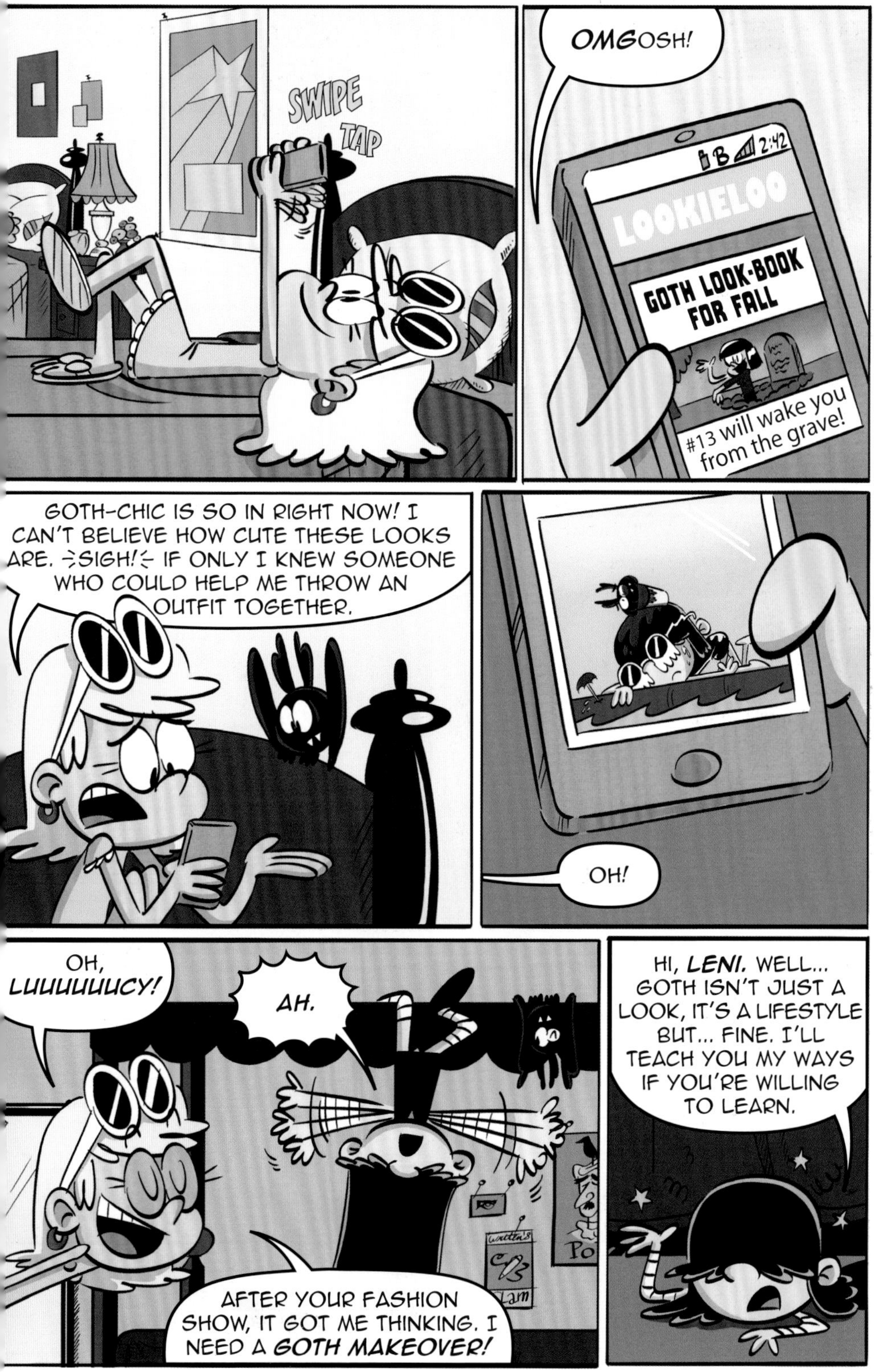
SWIPE
TAP
OMGOSH!
LOOKIELOO
GOTH LOOK-BOOK FOR FALL
#13 will wake you from the grave!
GOTH-CHIC IS SO IN RIGHT NOW! I CAN'T BELIEVE HOW CUTE THESE LOOKS ARE. SIGH! IF ONLY I KNEW SOMEONE WHO COULD HELP ME THROW AN OUTFIT TOGETHER.
OH!
OH, LUUUUUUCY!
AH.
AFTER YOUR FASHION SHOW, IT GOT ME THINKING. I NEED A GOTH MAKEOVER!
HI, LENI. WELL... GOTH ISN'T JUST A LOOK, IT'S A LIFESTYLE BUT... FINE. I'LL TEACH YOU MY WAYS IF YOU'RE WILLING TO LEARN.

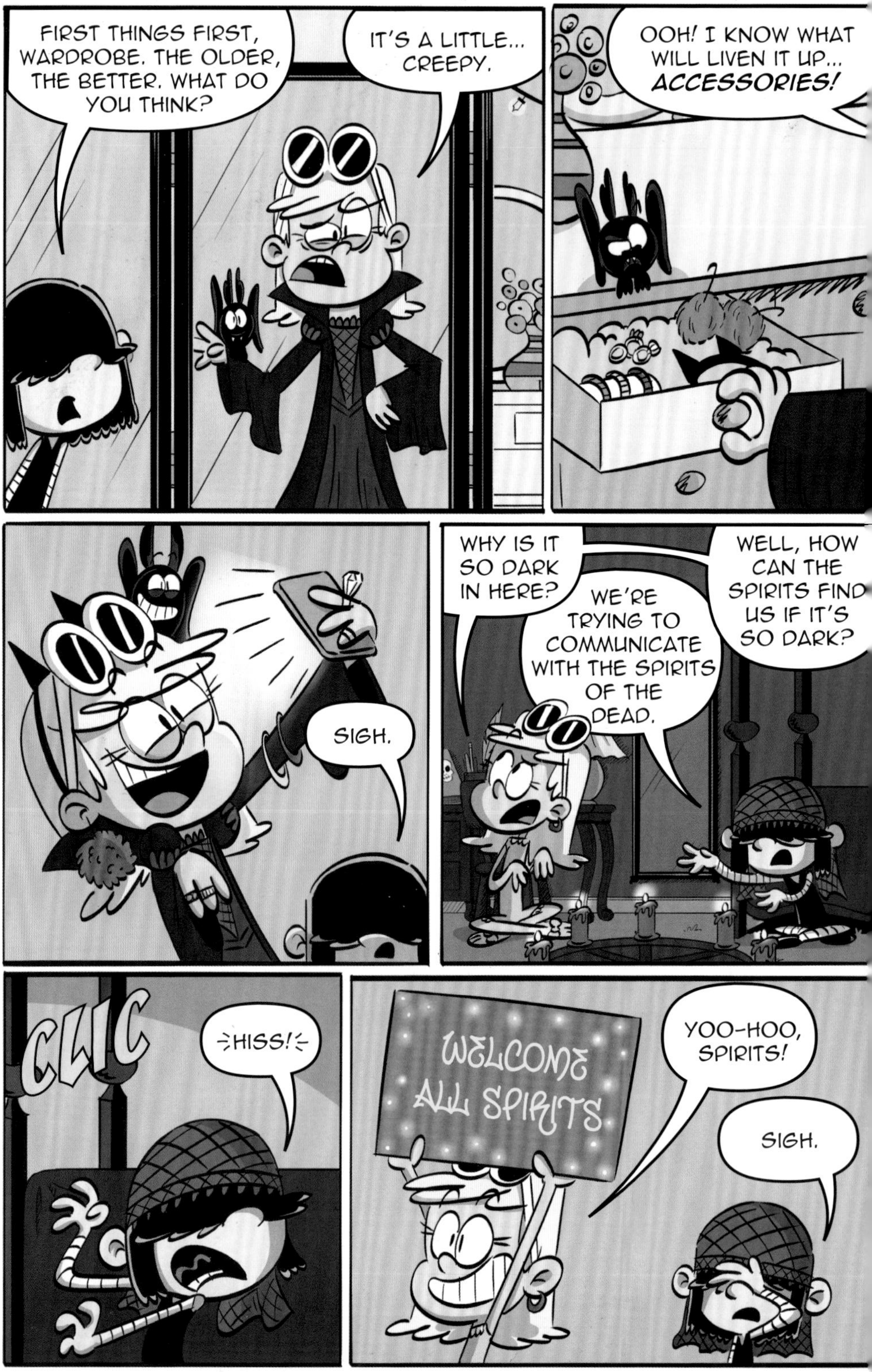
FIRST THINGS FIRST, WARDROBE. THE OLDER, THE BETTER. WHAT DO YOU THINK?
IT'S A LITTLE... CREEPY.
OOH! I KNOW WHAT WILL LIVEN IT UP... ACCESSORIES!
SIGH.
WHY IS IT SO DARK IN HERE?
WE'RE TRYING TO COMMUNICATE WITH THE SPIRITS OF THE DEAD.
WELL, HOW CAN THE SPIRITS FIND US IF IT'S SO DARK?
CLIC
HISS!
WELCOME ALL SPIRITS
YOO-HOO, SPIRITS!
SIGH.

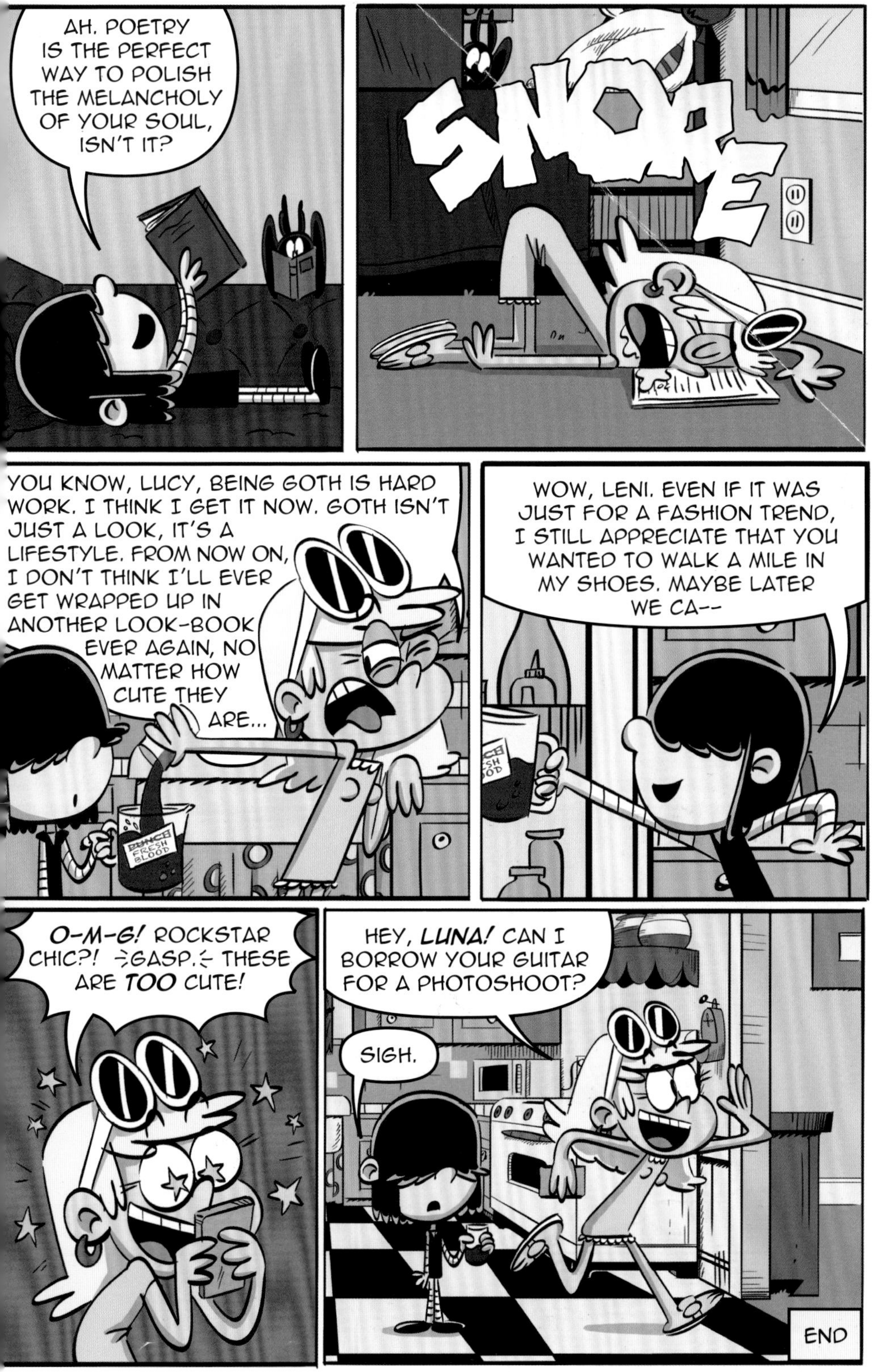
AH. POETRY IS THE PERFECT WAY TO POLISH THE MELANCHOLY OF YOUR SOUL, ISN'T IT?
SNORE
YOU KNOW, LUCY, BEING GOTH IS HARD WORK. I THINK I GET IT NOW. GOTH ISN'T JUST A LOOK, IT'S A LIFESTYLE. FROM NOW ON, I DON'T THINK I'LL EVER GET WRAPPED UP IN ANOTHER LOOK-BOOK EVER AGAIN, NO MATTER HOW CUTE THEY ARE...
FRESH BLOOD
WOW, LENI. EVEN IF IT WAS JUST FOR A FASHION TREND, I STILL APPRECIATE THAT YOU WANTED TO WALK A MILE IN MY SHOES. MAYBE LATER WE CA--
O-M-G! ROCKSTAR CHIC?! GASP. THESE ARE TOO CUTE!
HEY, LUNA! CAN I BORROW YOUR GUITAR FOR A PHOTOSHOOT?
SIGH.
END

"LINCOLN'S SURVIVAL GUIDE"

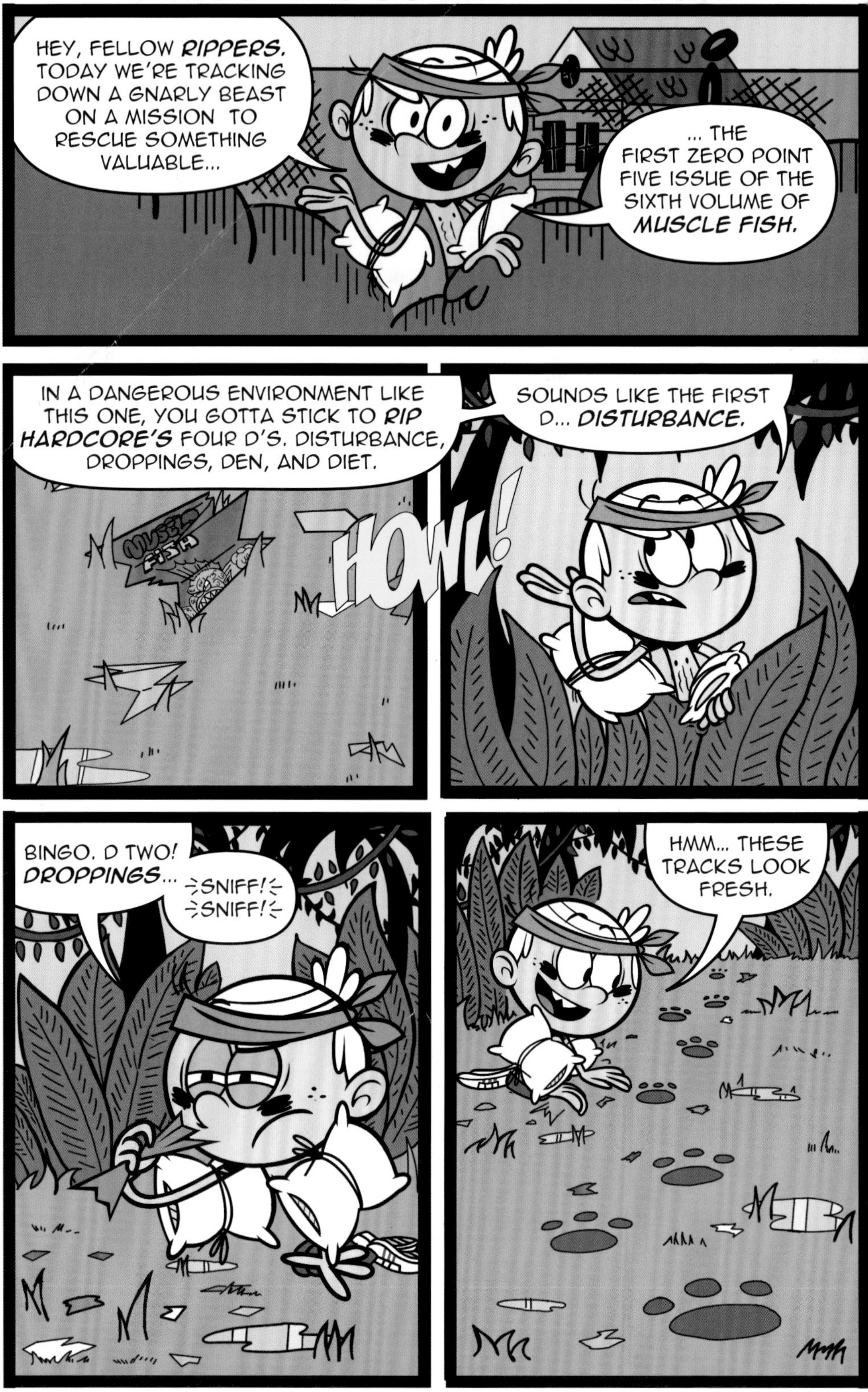
HEY, FELLOW RIPPERS. TODAY WE'RE TRACKING DOWN A GNARLY BEAST ON A MISSION TO RESCUE SOMETHING VALUABLE...
... THE FIRST ZERO POINT FIVE ISSUE OF THE SIXTH VOLUME OF MUSCLE FISH.
IN A DANGEROUS ENVIRONMENT LIKE THIS ONE, YOU GOTTA STICK TO RIP HARDCORE'S FOUR D'S. DISTURBANCE, DROPPINGS, DEN, AND DIET.
HOWL!
SOUNDS LIKE THE FIRST D... DISTURBANCE.
BINGO. D TWO! DROPPINGS...
SNIFF! SNIFF!
HMM... THESE TRACKS LOOK FRESH.

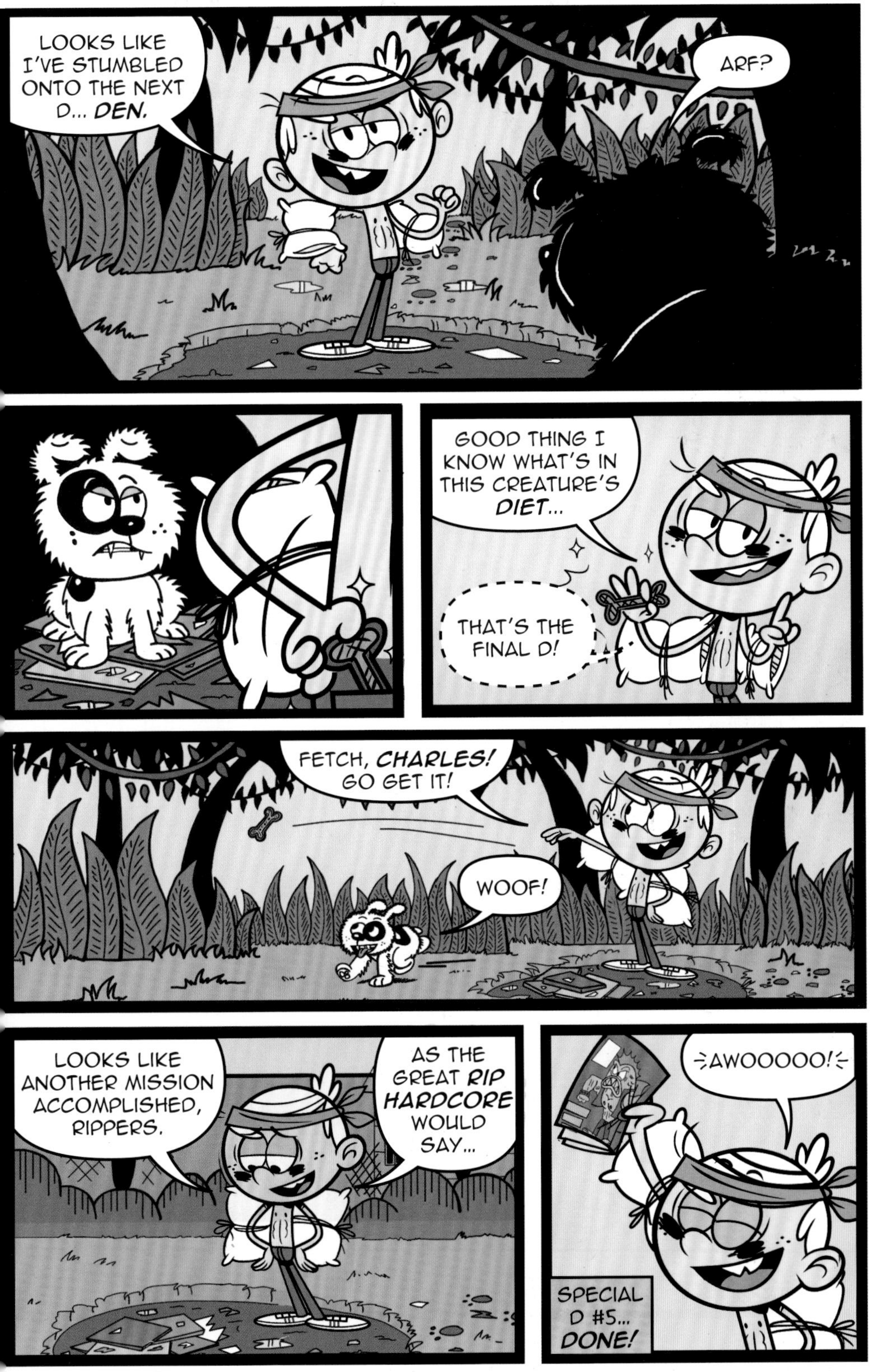
LOOKS LIKE I'VE STUMBLED ONTO THE NEXT D... DEN.
ARF?
GOOD THING I KNOW WHAT'S IN THIS CREATURE'S DIET...
THAT'S THE FINAL D!
FETCH, CHARLES! GO GET IT!
WOOF!
LOOKS LIKE ANOTHER MISSION ACCOMPLISHED, RIPPERS.
AS THE GREAT RIP HARDCORE WOULD SAY...
AWOOOOO!
SPECIAL D #5... DONE!

"EVEN THE SCORE"

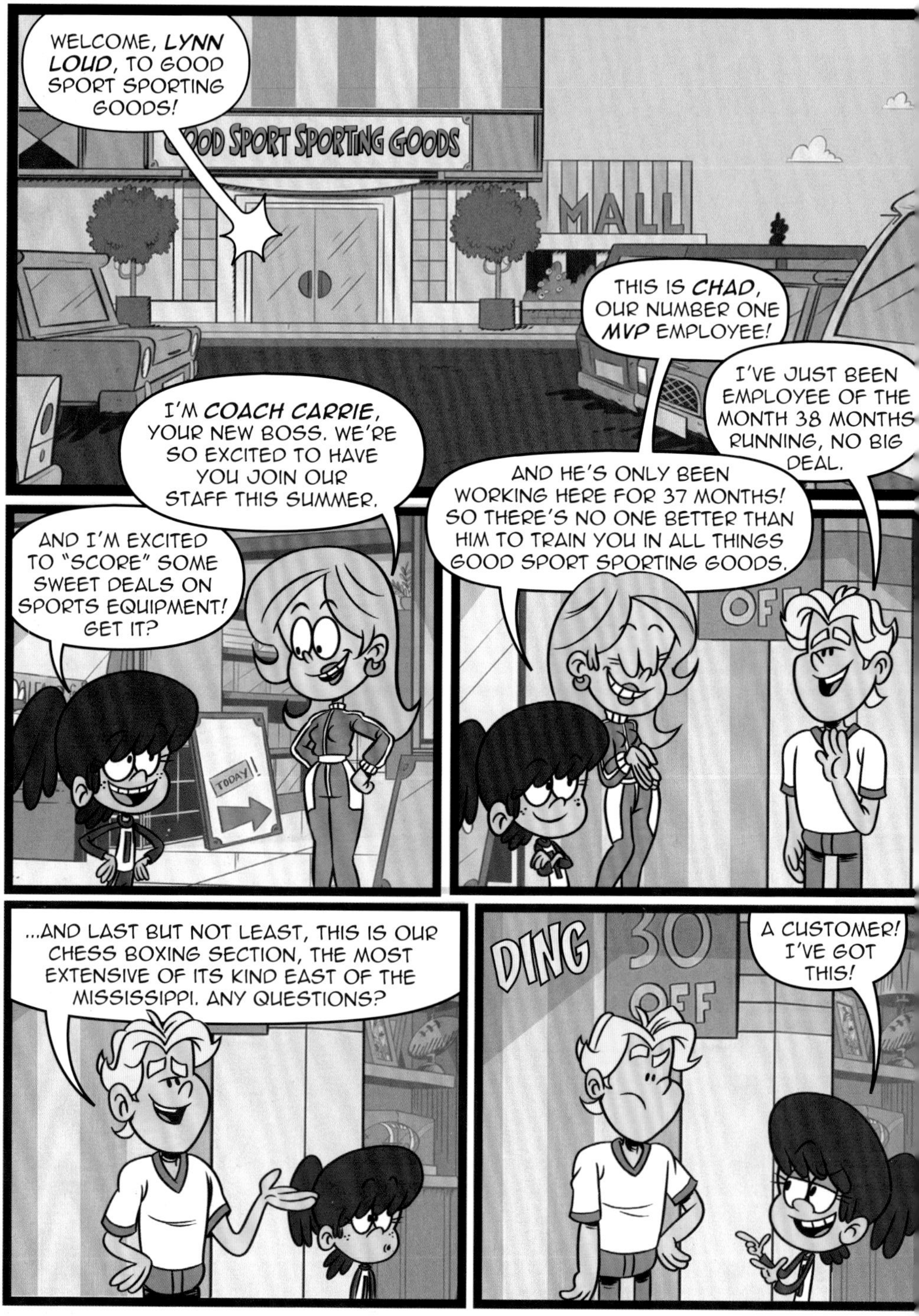
WELCOME, LYNN LOUD, TO GOOD SPORT SPORTING GOODS!
GOOD SPORT SPORTING GOODS
MALL
I'M COACH CARRIE, YOUR NEW BOSS. WE'RE SO EXCITED TO HAVE YOU JOIN OUR STAFF THIS SUMMER.
AND I'M EXCITED TO "SCORE" SOME SWEET DEALS ON SPORTS EQUIPMENT! GET IT?
TODAY!
THIS IS CHAD, OUR NUMBER ONE MVP EMPLOYEE!
I'VE JUST BEEN EMPLOYEE OF THE MONTH 38 MONTHS RUNNING, NO BIG DEAL.
AND HE'S ONLY BEEN WORKING HERE FOR 37 MONTHS! SO THERE'S NO ONE BETTER THAN HIM TO TRAIN YOU IN ALL THINGS GOOD SPORT SPORTING GOODS.
...AND LAST BUT NOT LEAST, THIS IS OUR CHESS BOXING SECTION, THE MOST EXTENSIVE OF ITS KIND EAST OF THE MISSISSIPPI. ANY QUESTIONS?
DING
30 OFF
A CUSTOMER! I'VE GOT THIS!

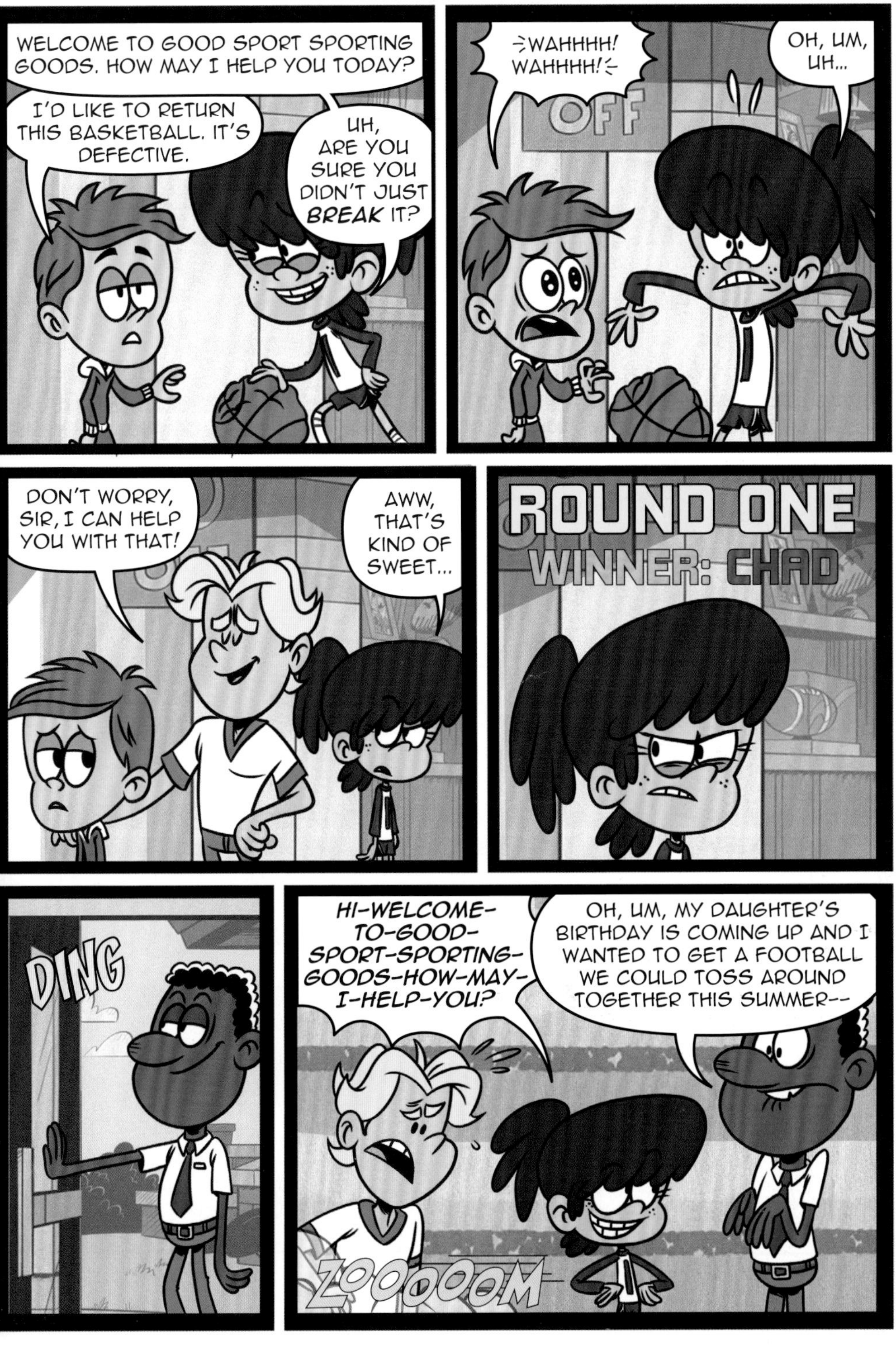
WELCOME TO GOOD SPORT SPORTING GOODS. HOW MAY I HELP YOU TODAY?
I'D LIKE TO RETURN THIS BASKETBALL. IT'S DEFECTIVE.
UH, ARE YOU SURE YOU DIDN'T JUST *BREAK* IT?
WAHHHH! WAHHHH!
OH, UM, UH...
DON'T WORRY, SIR, I CAN HELP YOU WITH THAT!
AWW, THAT'S KIND OF SWEET...
ROUND ONE
WINNER: CHAD
DING
HI-WELCOME-TO-GOOD-SPORT-SPORTING-GOODS-HOW-MAY-I-HELP-YOU?
OH, UM, MY DAUGHTER'S BIRTHDAY IS COMING UP AND I WANTED TO GET A FOOTBALL WE COULD TOSS AROUND TOGETHER THIS SUMMER--
ZOOOOOM

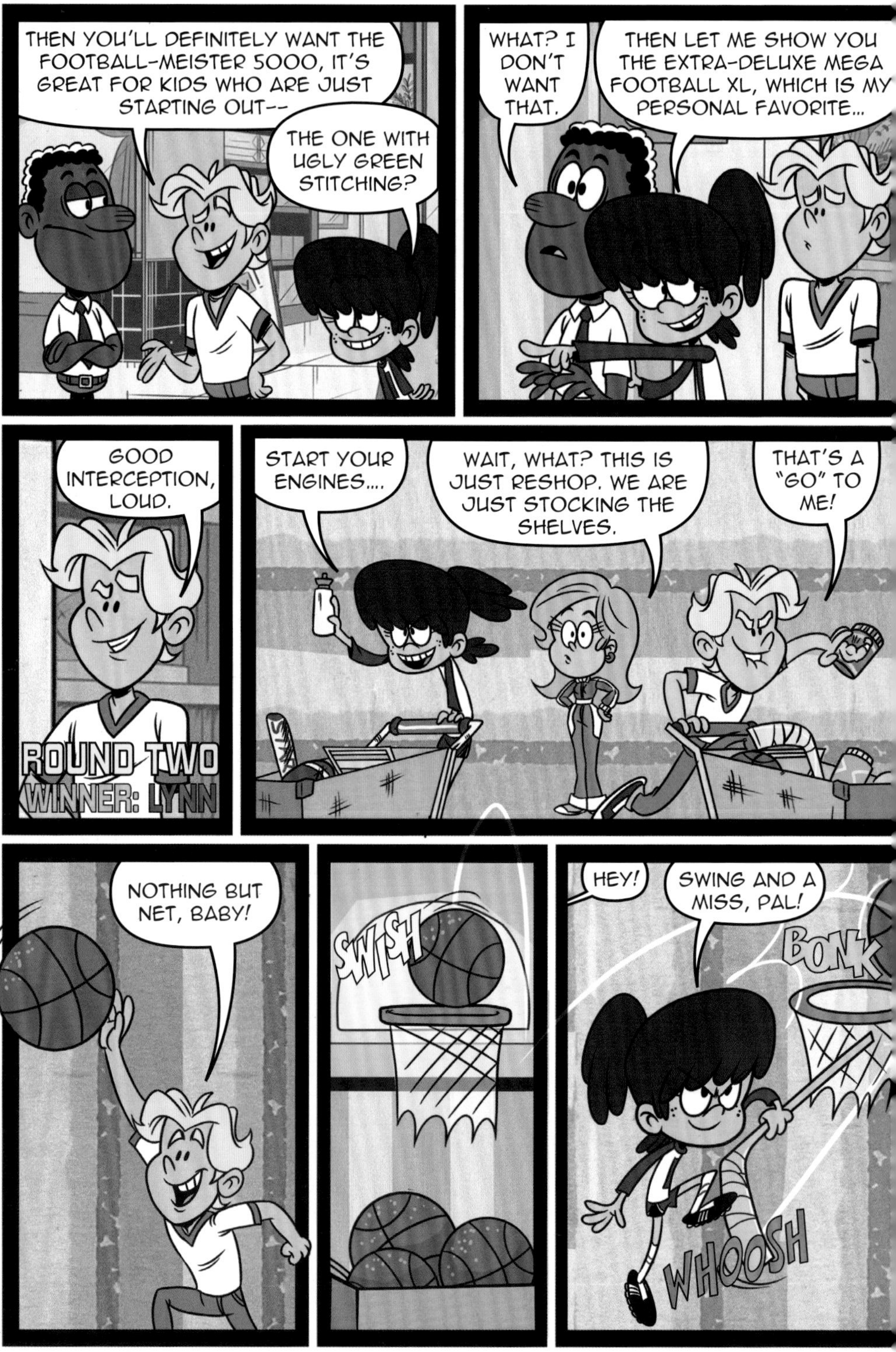
THEN YOU'LL DEFINITELY WANT THE FOOTBALL-MEISTER 5000, IT'S GREAT FOR KIDS WHO ARE JUST STARTING OUT--
THE ONE WITH UGLY GREEN STITCHING?
WHAT? I DON'T WANT THAT.
THEN LET ME SHOW YOU THE EXTRA-DELUXE MEGA FOOTBALL XL, WHICH IS MY PERSONAL FAVORITE...
GOOD INTERCEPTION, LOUD.
ROUND TWO
WINNER: LYNN
START YOUR ENGINES....
WAIT, WHAT? THIS IS JUST RESHOP. WE ARE JUST STOCKING THE SHELVES.
THAT'S A "GO" TO ME!
NOTHING BUT NET, BABY!
SWISH
HEY!
SWING AND A MISS, PAL!
BONK
WHOOSH

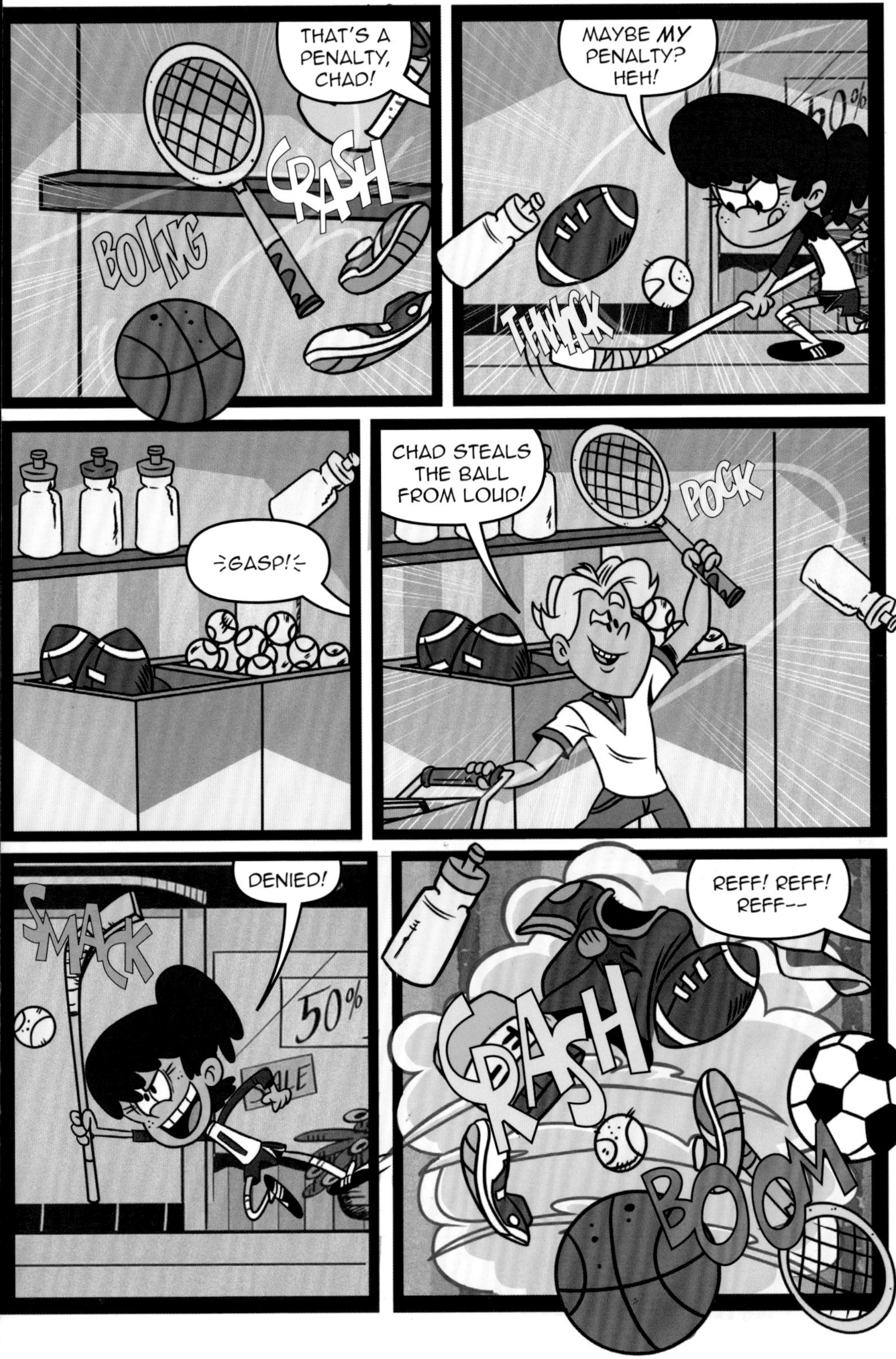
THAT'S A PENALTY, CHAD!
CRASH
BOING
MAYBE MY PENALTY? HEH!
50%
THWACK
CHAD STEALS THE BALL FROM LOUD!
POCK
GASP!
DENIED!
SMACK
50%
SALE
REFF! REFF! REFF--
CRASH
BOOM

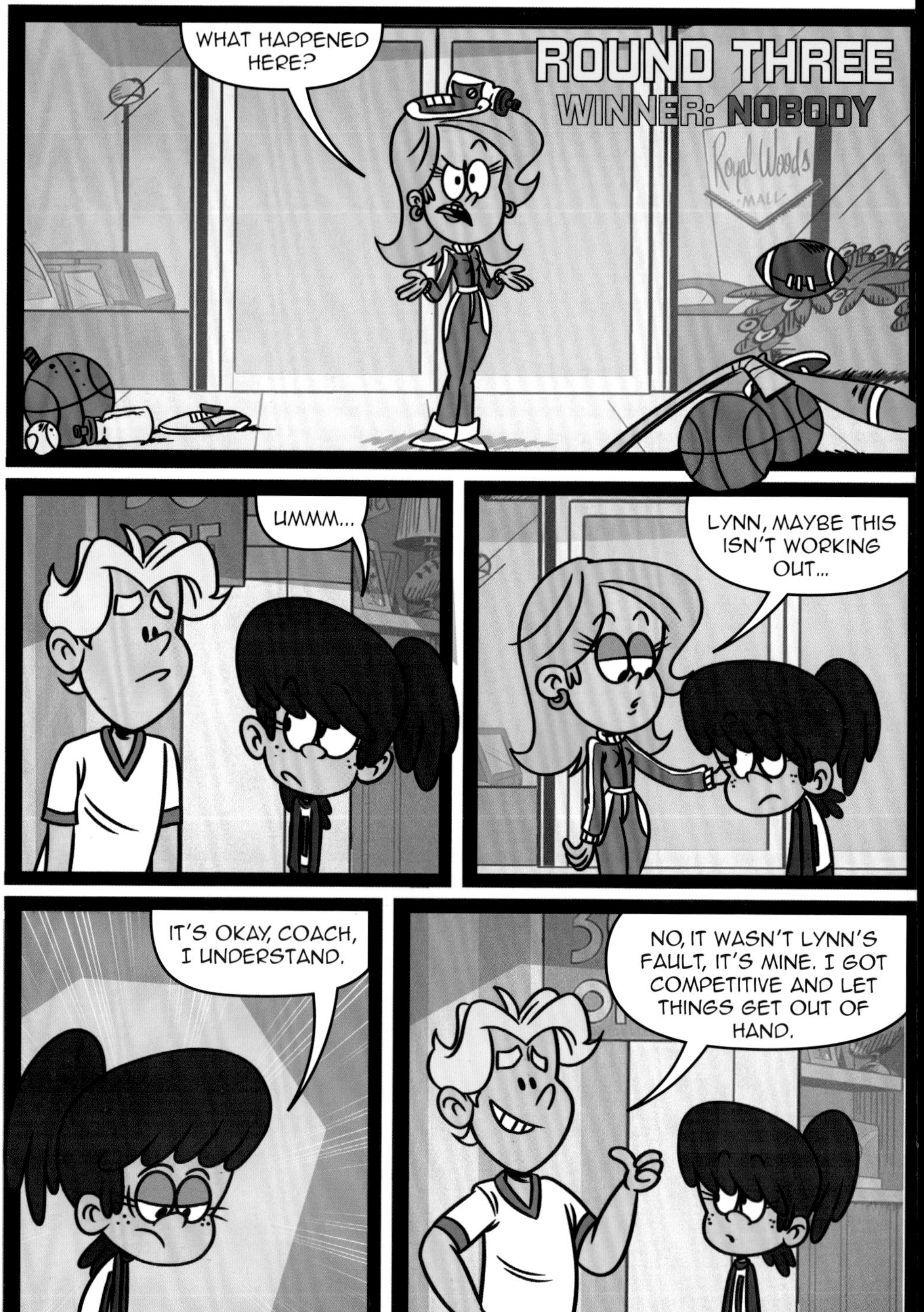
ROUND THREE
WINNER: NOBODY
WHAT HAPPENED HERE?
Royal Woods MALL
UMMM...
LYNN, MAYBE THIS ISN'T WORKING OUT...
IT'S OKAY, COACH, I UNDERSTAND.
NO, IT WASN'T LYNN'S FAULT, IT'S MINE. I GOT COMPETITIVE AND LET THINGS GET OUT OF HAND.

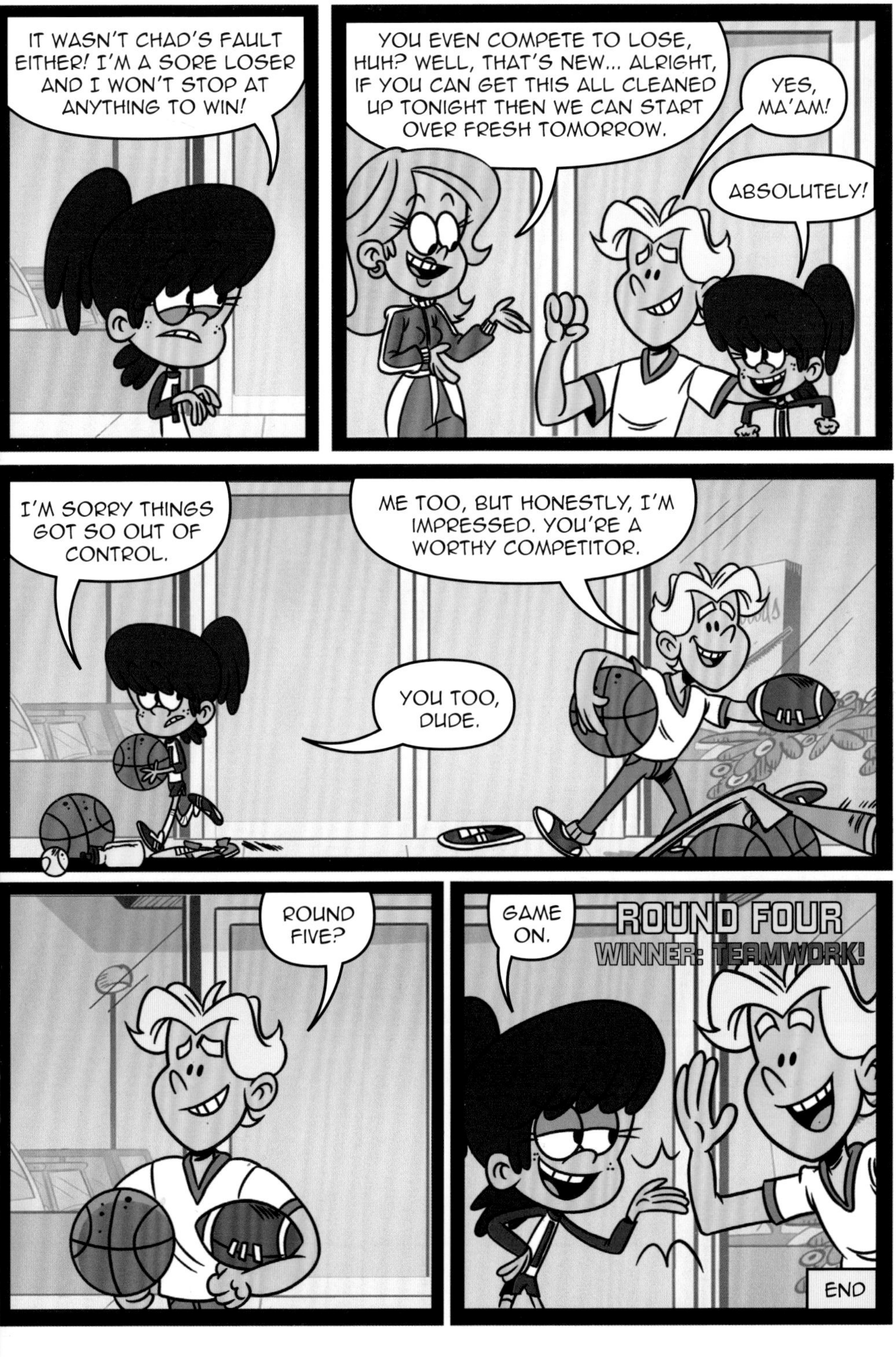
IT WASN'T CHAD'S FAULT EITHER! I'M A SORE LOSER AND I WON'T STOP AT ANYTHING TO WIN!
YOU EVEN COMPETE TO LOSE, HUH? WELL, THAT'S NEW... ALRIGHT, IF YOU CAN GET THIS ALL CLEANED UP TONIGHT THEN WE CAN START OVER FRESH TOMORROW.
YES, MA'AM!
ABSOLUTELY!
I'M SORRY THINGS GOT SO OUT OF CONTROL.
ME TOO, BUT HONESTLY, I'M IMPRESSED. YOU'RE A WORTHY COMPETITOR.
YOU TOO, DUDE.
ROUND FIVE?
GAME ON.
ROUND FOUR
WINNER: TEAMWORK!
END

"TUNNEL OF MUD"

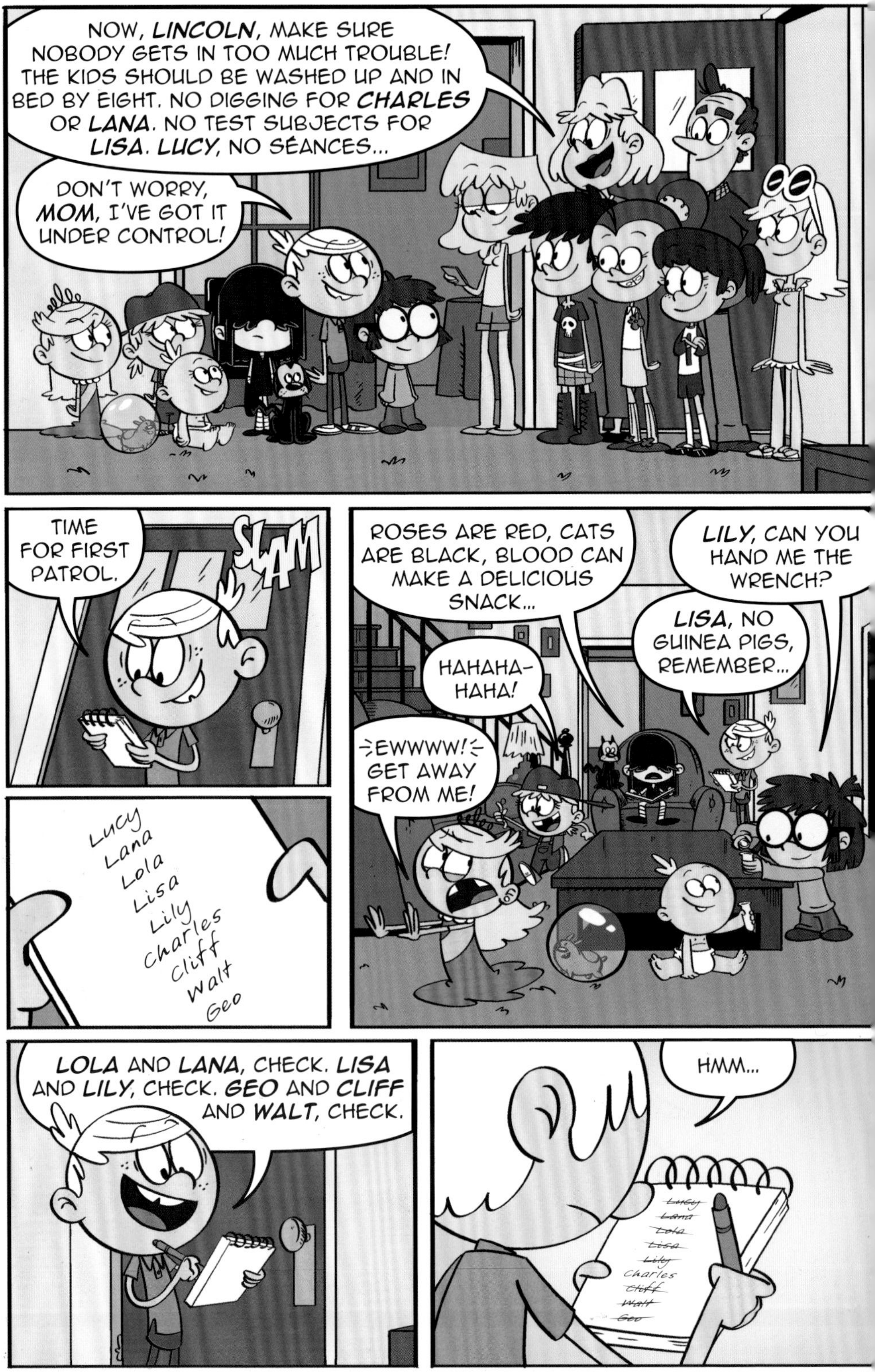

NOW, LINCOLN, MAKE SURE NOBODY GETS IN TOO MUCH TROUBLE! THE KIDS SHOULD BE WASHED UP AND IN BED BY EIGHT. NO DIGGING FOR CHARLES OR LANA. NO TEST SUBJECTS FOR LISA. LUCY, NO SÉANCES...
DON'T WORRY, MOM, I'VE GOT IT UNDER CONTROL!
TIME FOR FIRST PATROL.
SLAM
Lucy
Lana
Lola
Lisa
Lily
Charles
Cliff
Walt
Geo
ROSES ARE RED, CATS ARE BLACK, BLOOD CAN MAKE A DELICIOUS SNACK...
LILY, CAN YOU HAND ME THE WRENCH?
HAHAHA-HAHA!
LISA, NO GUINEA PIGS, REMEMBER...
EWWWW! GET AWAY FROM ME!
LOLA AND LANA, CHECK. LISA AND LILY, CHECK. GEO AND CLIFF AND WALT, CHECK.
HMM...
~~Lucy~~
~~Lana~~
~~Lola~~
~~Lisa~~
~~Lily~~
Charles
~~Cliff~~
~~Walt~~
~~Geo~~

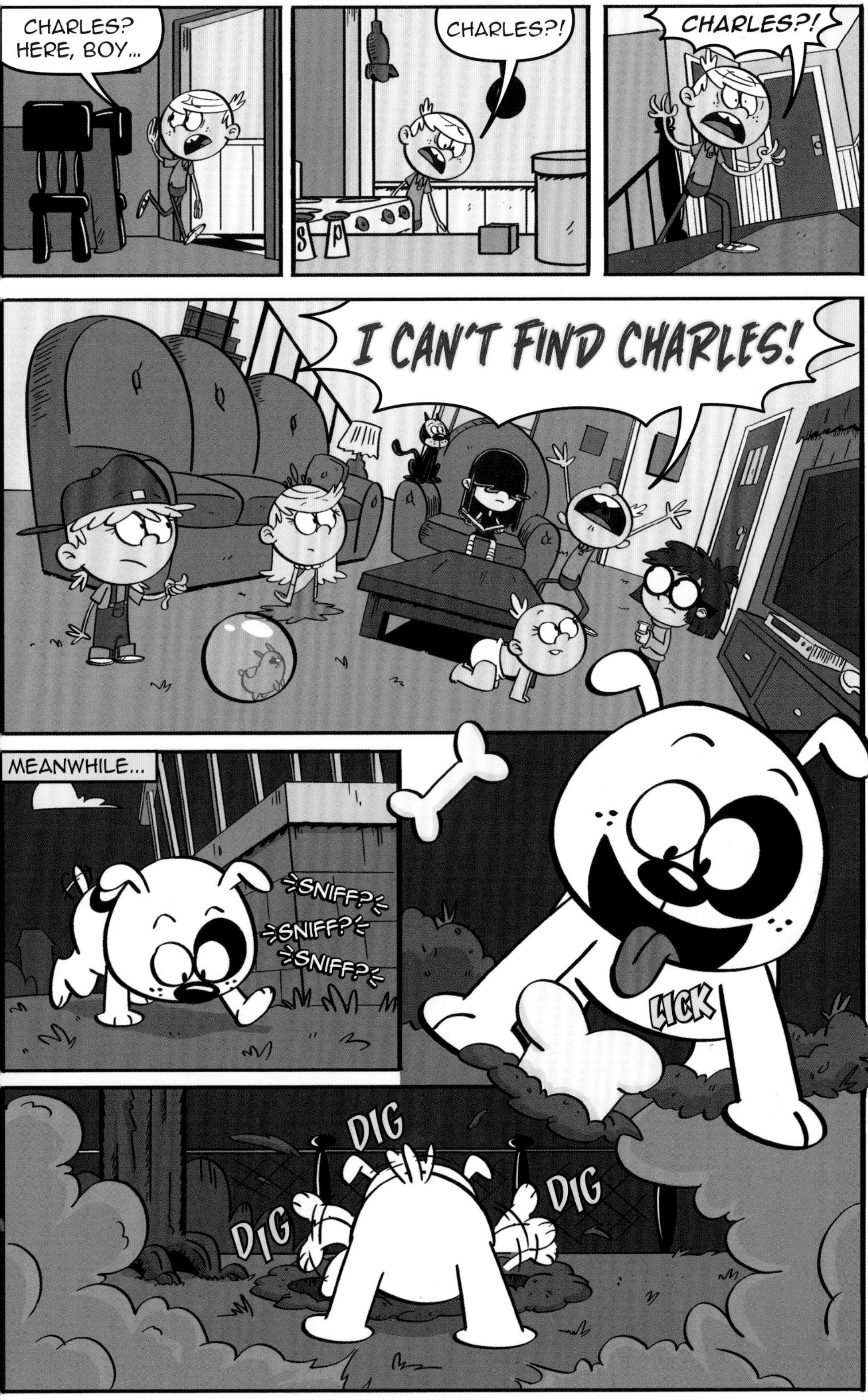

CHARLES? HERE, BOY...
CHARLES?!
CHARLES?!
I CAN'T FIND CHARLES!
MEANWHILE...
SNIFF?
SNIFF?
SNIFF?
LICK
DIG
DIG
DIG

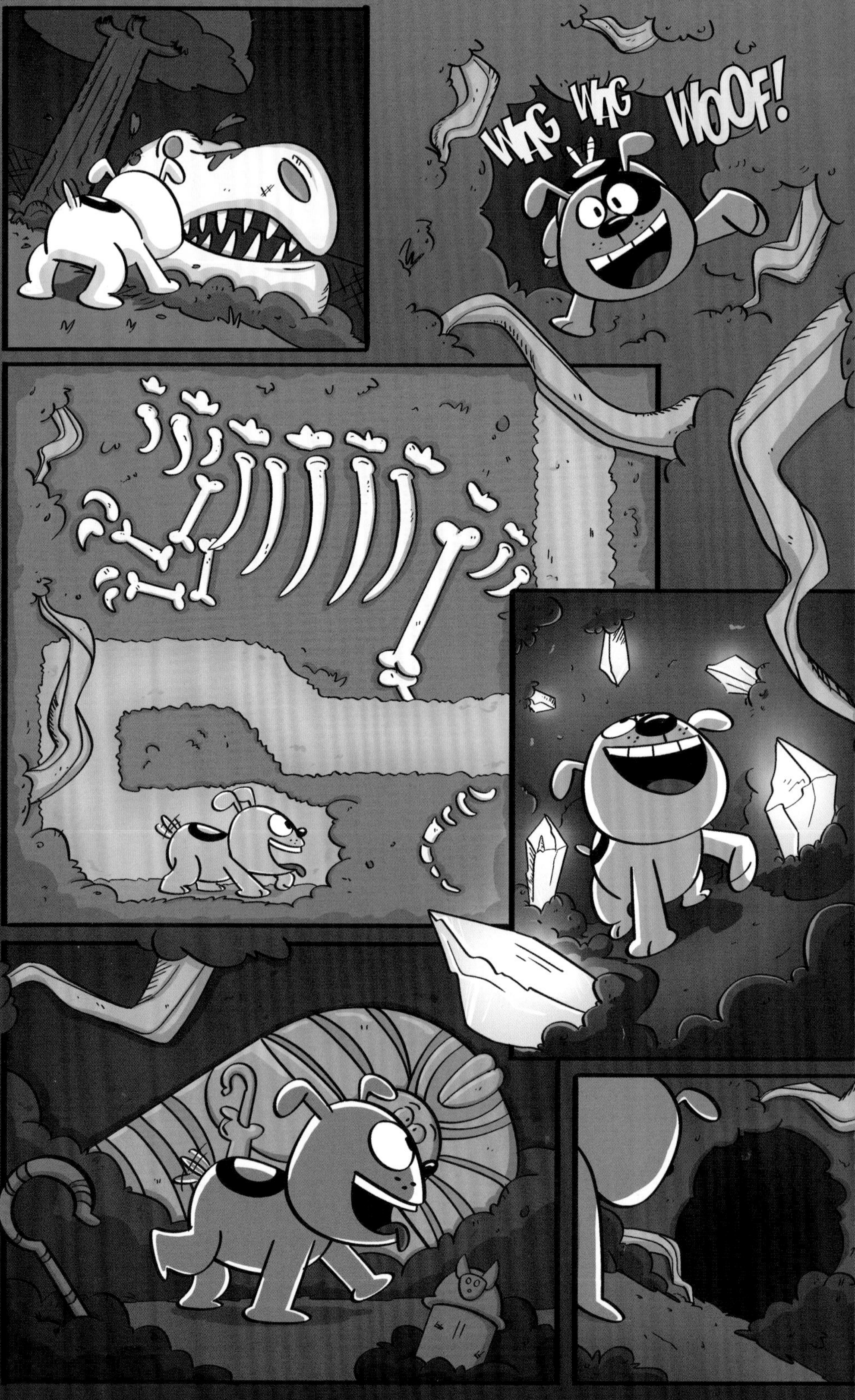
WAG WAG
WOOF!

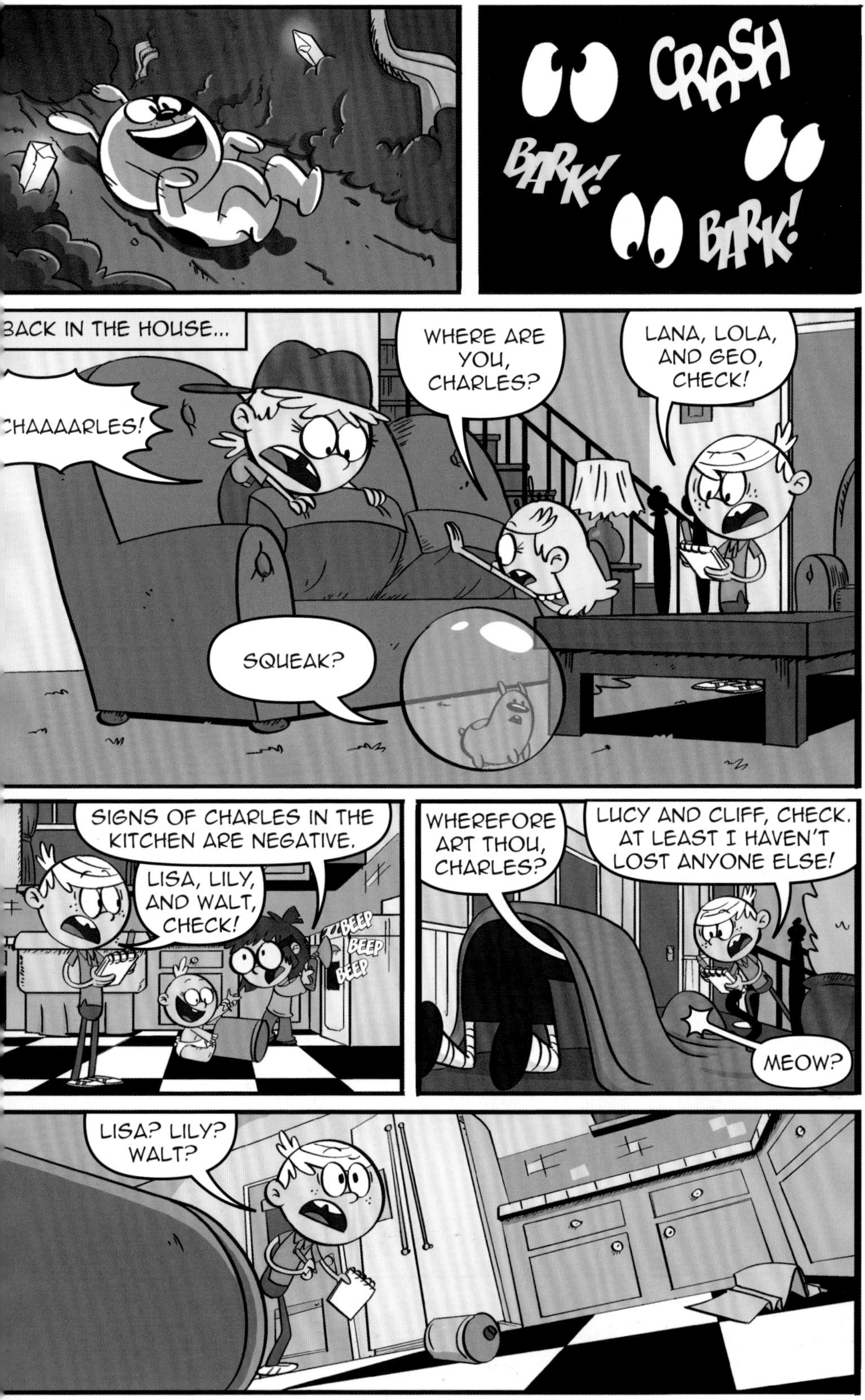
CRASH
BARK!
BARK!
BACK IN THE HOUSE...
CHAAAARLES!
WHERE ARE YOU, CHARLES?
LANA, LOLA, AND GEO, CHECK!
SQUEAK?
SIGNS OF CHARLES IN THE KITCHEN ARE NEGATIVE.
LISA, LILY, AND WALT, CHECK!
BEEP
BEEP
BEEP
WHEREFORE ART THOU, CHARLES?
LUCY AND CLIFF, CHECK. AT LEAST I HAVEN'T LOST ANYONE ELSE!
MEOW?
LISA? LILY? WALT?

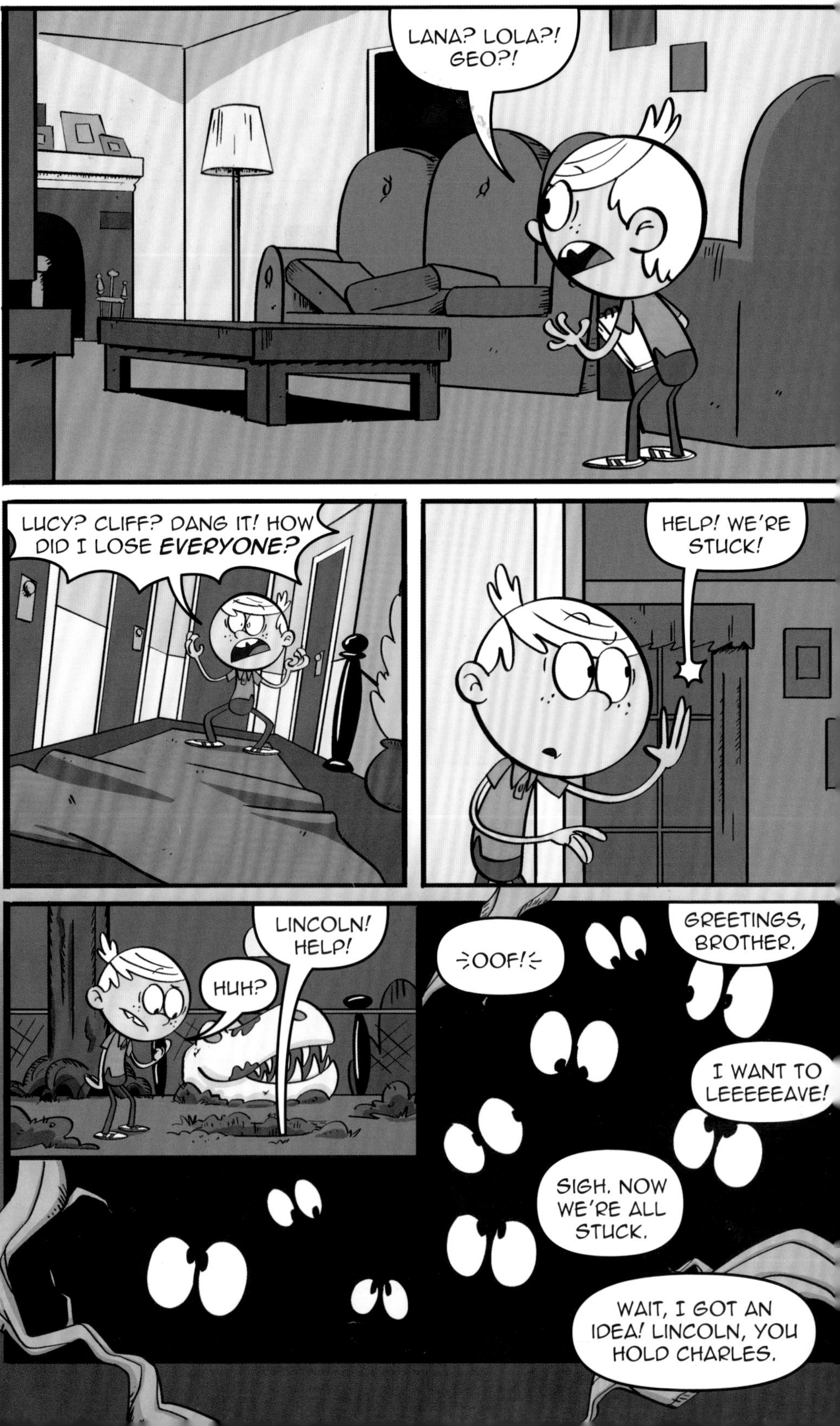
LANA? LOLA?!
GEO?!
LUCY? CLIFF? DANG IT! HOW DID I LOSE **EVERYONE?**
HELP! WE'RE STUCK!
LINCOLN! HELP!
HUH?
OOF!
GREETINGS, BROTHER.
I WANT TO LEEEEEAVE!
SIGH. NOW WE'RE ALL STUCK.
WAIT, I GOT AN IDEA! LINCOLN, YOU HOLD CHARLES.

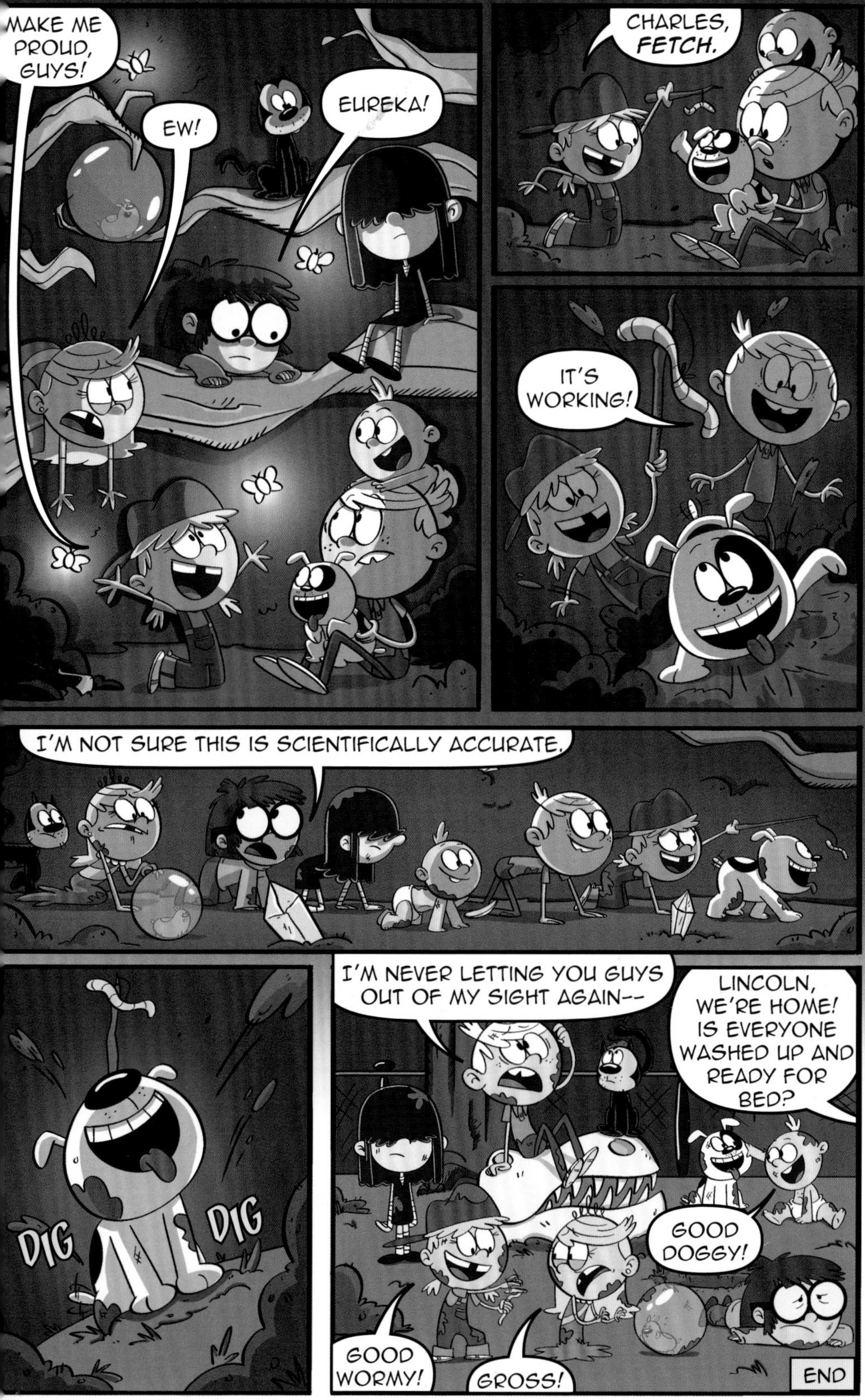
MAKE ME PROUD, GUYS!
EW!
EUREKA!
CHARLES, FETCH.
IT'S WORKING!
I'M NOT SURE THIS IS SCIENTIFICALLY ACCURATE.
DIG
DIG
I'M NEVER LETTING YOU GUYS OUT OF MY SIGHT AGAIN--
LINCOLN, WE'RE HOME! IS EVERYONE WASHED UP AND READY FOR BED?
GOOD DOGGY!
GOOD WORMY!
GROSS!
END

"LUNCH ON THE RUN"

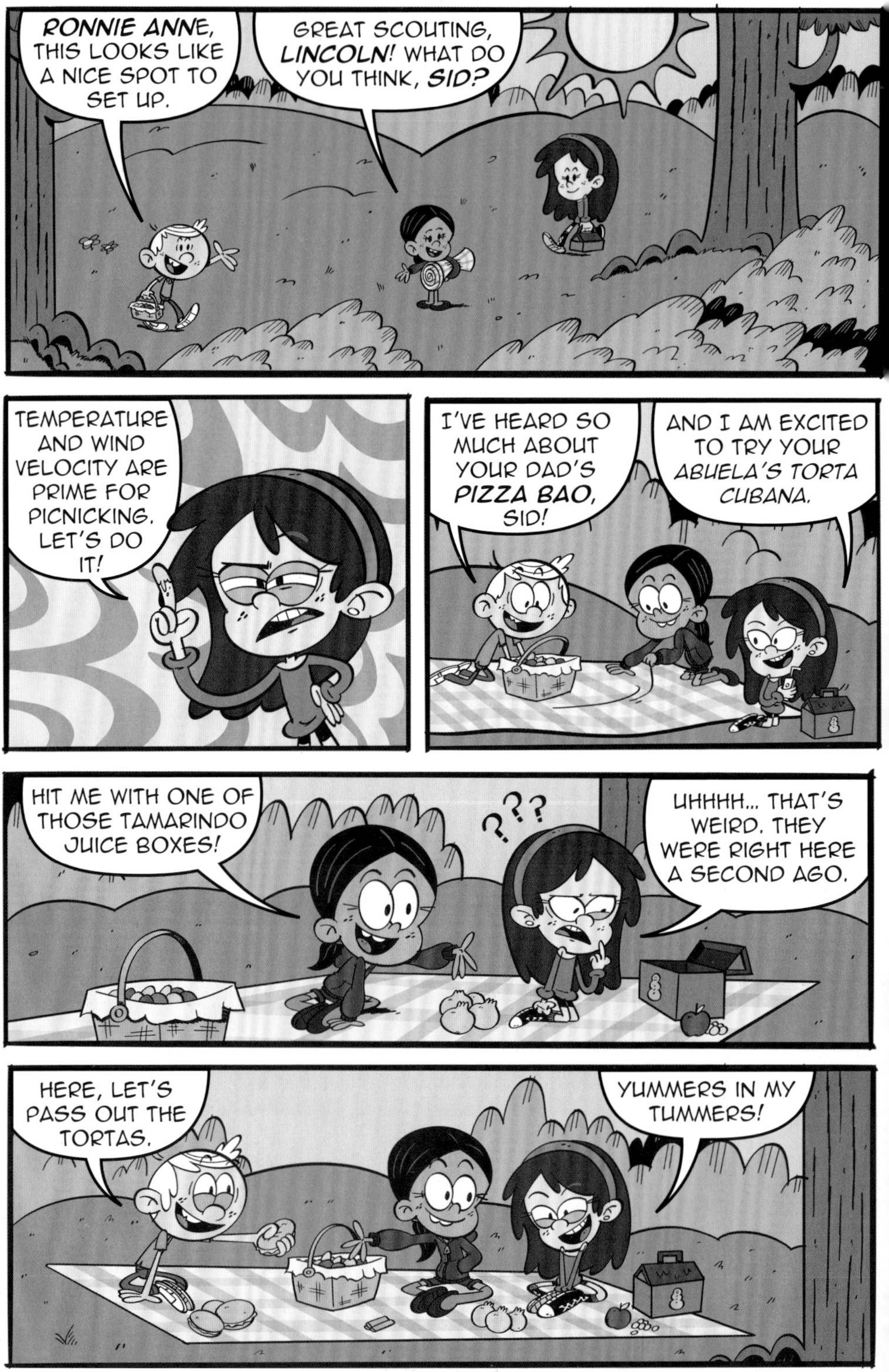
RONNIE ANNE, THIS LOOKS LIKE A NICE SPOT TO SET UP.
GREAT SCOUTING, LINCOLN! WHAT DO YOU THINK, SID?
TEMPERATURE AND WIND VELOCITY ARE PRIME FOR PICNICKING. LET'S DO IT!
I'VE HEARD SO MUCH ABOUT YOUR DAD'S PIZZA BAO, SID!
AND I AM EXCITED TO TRY YOUR ABUELA'S TORTA CUBANA.
HIT ME WITH ONE OF THOSE TAMARINDO JUICE BOXES!
???
UHHHH... THAT'S WEIRD. THEY WERE RIGHT HERE A SECOND AGO.
HERE, LET'S PASS OUT THE TORTAS.
YUMMERS IN MY TUMMERS!

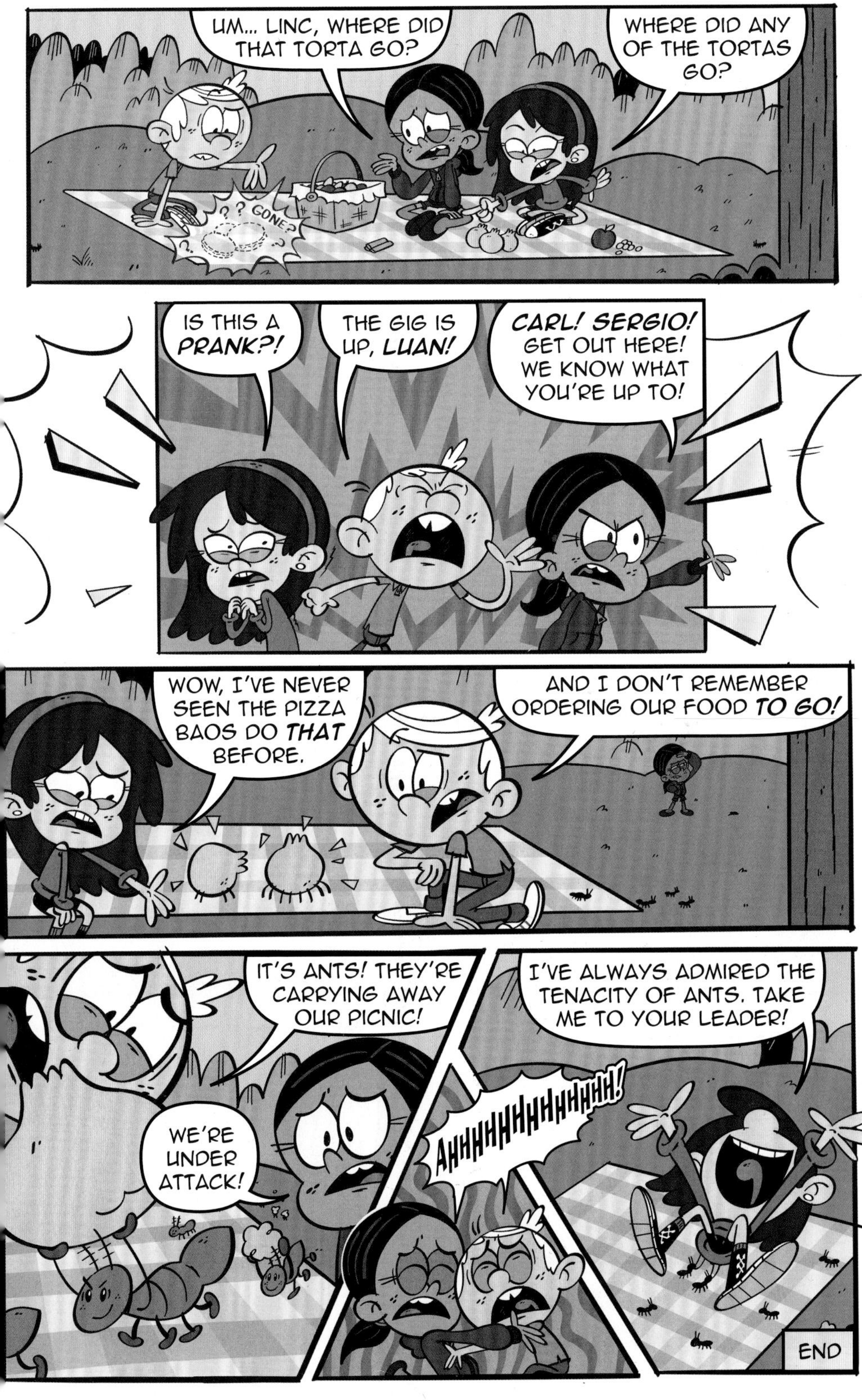
UM... LINC, WHERE DID THAT TORTA GO?
WHERE DID ANY OF THE TORTAS GO?
? ? GONE?
IS THIS A PRANK?!
THE GIG IS UP, LUAN!
CARL! SERGIO! GET OUT HERE! WE KNOW WHAT YOU'RE UP TO!
WOW, I'VE NEVER SEEN THE PIZZA BAOS DO THAT BEFORE.
AND I DON'T REMEMBER ORDERING OUR FOOD TO GO!
IT'S ANTS! THEY'RE CARRYING AWAY OUR PICNIC!
WE'RE UNDER ATTACK!
I'VE ALWAYS ADMIRED THE TENACITY OF ANTS. TAKE ME TO YOUR LEADER!
AHHHHHHHHHHHHHH!
END

"SUNDAY IN THE PARK"

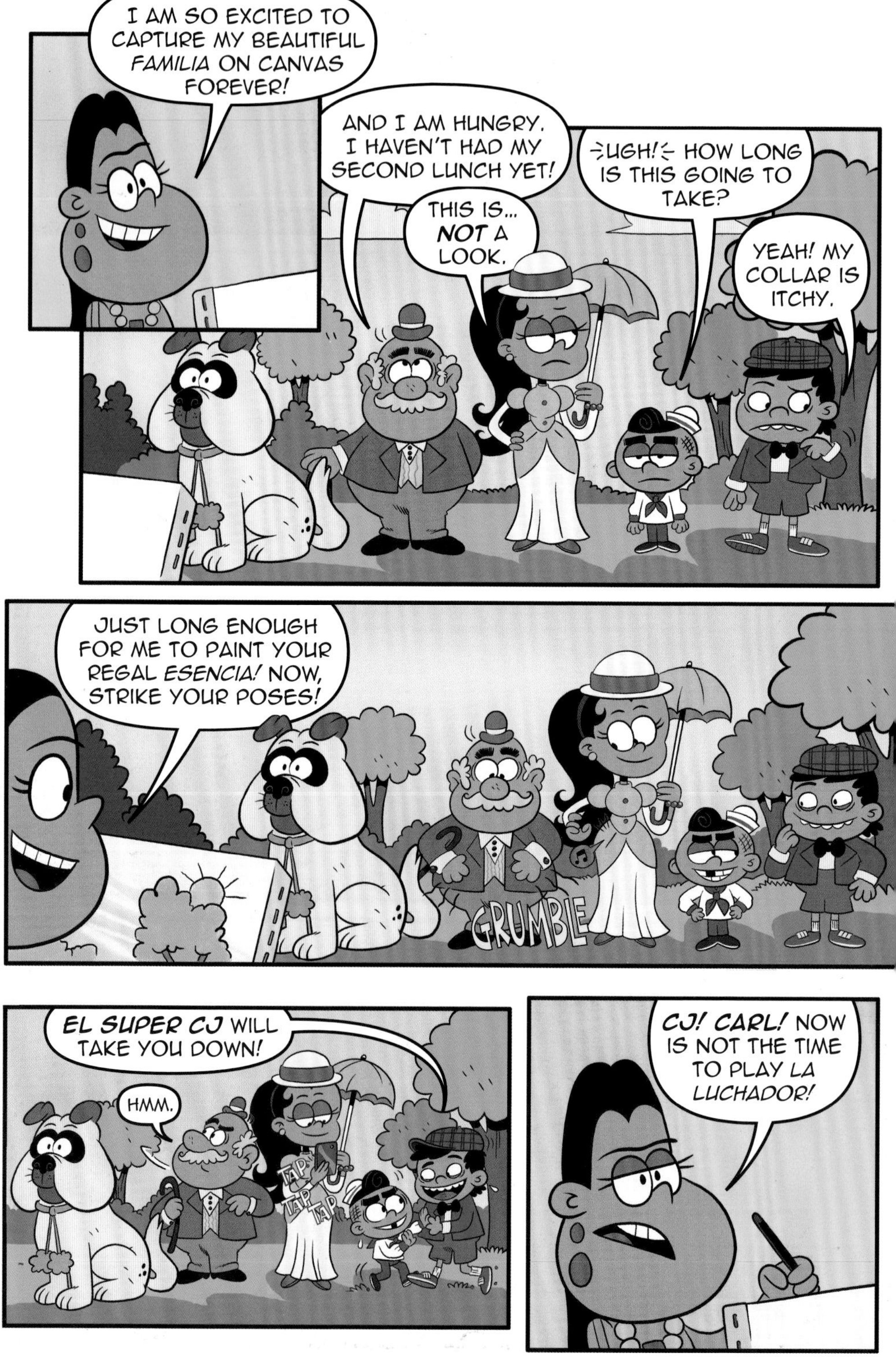

I AM SO EXCITED TO CAPTURE MY BEAUTIFUL *FAMILIA* ON CANVAS FOREVER!
AND I AM HUNGRY. I HAVEN'T HAD MY SECOND LUNCH YET!
THIS IS... ***NOT*** A LOOK.
UGH! HOW LONG IS THIS GOING TO TAKE?
YEAH! MY COLLAR IS ITCHY.
JUST LONG ENOUGH FOR ME TO PAINT YOUR REGAL *ESENCIA!* NOW, STRIKE YOUR POSES!
GRUMBLE
EL SUPER CJ WILL TAKE YOU DOWN!
HMM.
TAP TAP TAP
CJ! CARL! NOW IS NOT THE TIME TO PLAY *LA LUCHADOR!*

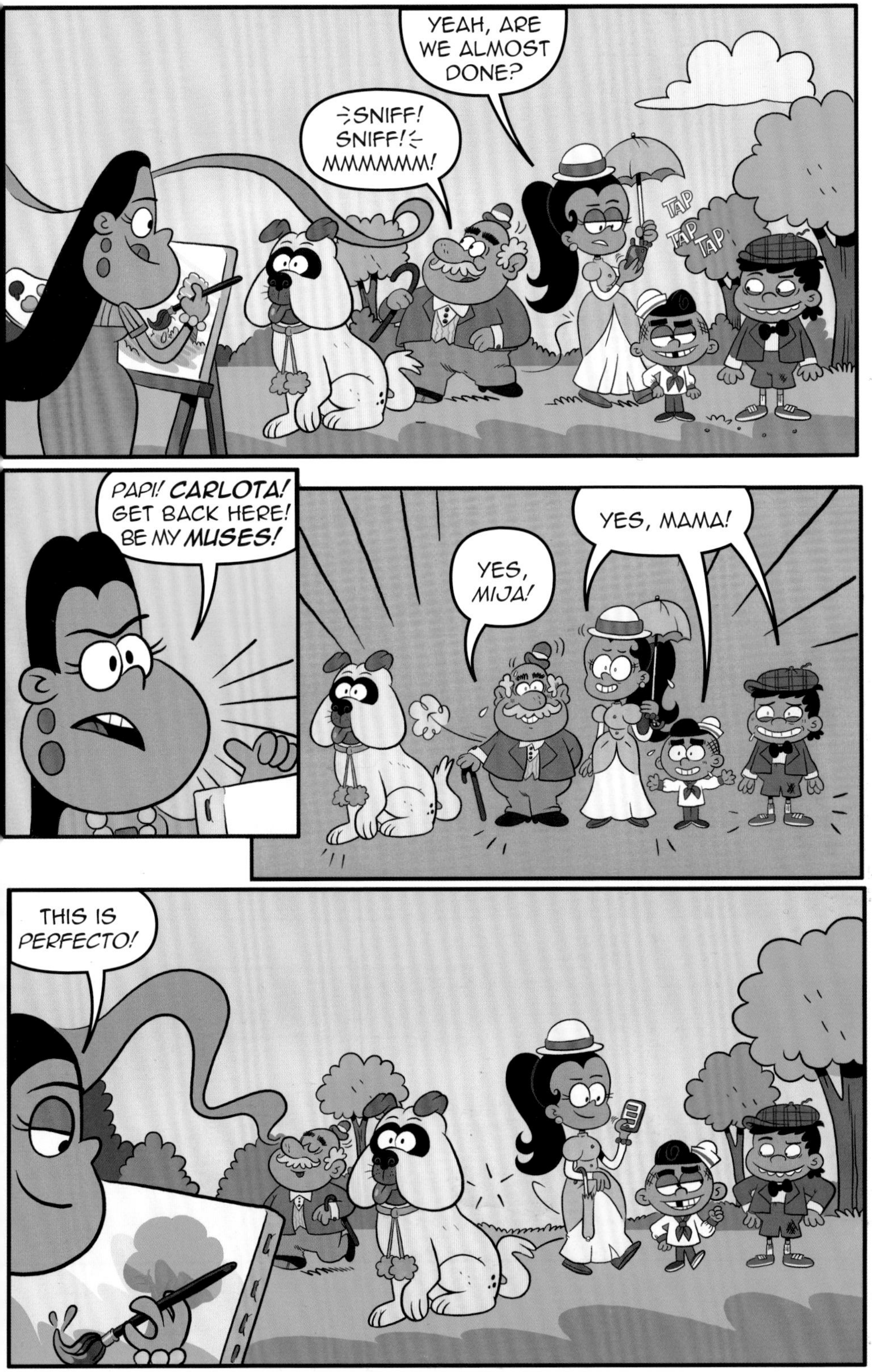
YEAH, ARE WE ALMOST DONE?
SNIFF! SNIFF! MMMMMMM!
TAP TAP TAP
PAPI! CARLOTA! GET BACK HERE! BE MY MUSES!
YES, MAMA!
YES, MIJA!
THIS IS PERFECTO!

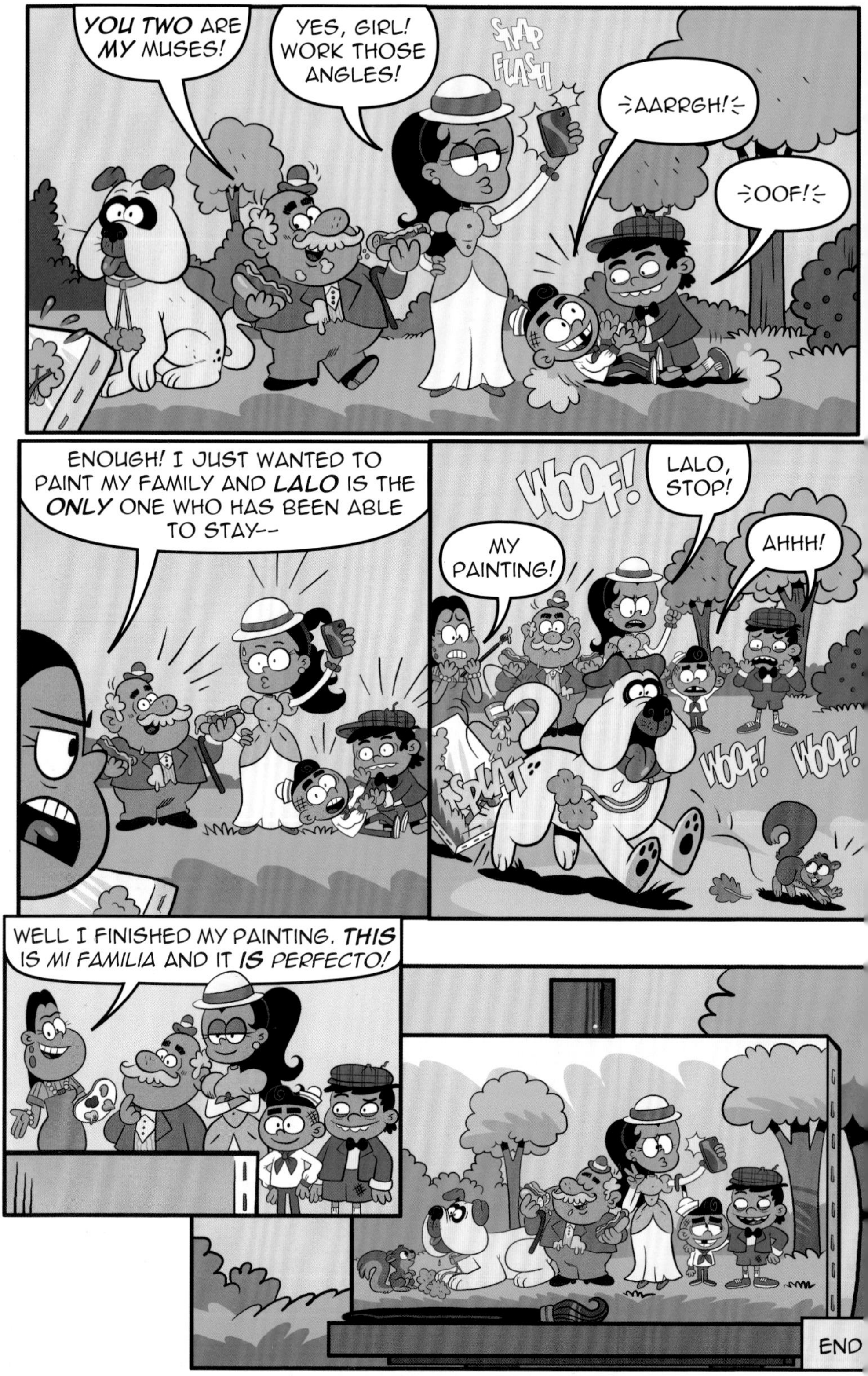
YOU TWO ARE MY MUSES!
YES, GIRL! WORK THOSE ANGLES!
SNAP
FLASH
AARRGH!
OOF!
ENOUGH! I JUST WANTED TO PAINT MY FAMILY AND LALO IS THE ONLY ONE WHO HAS BEEN ABLE TO STAY--
WOOF!
LALO, STOP!
MY PAINTING!
AHHH!
SPLAT!
WOOF! WOOF!
WELL I FINISHED MY PAINTING. THIS IS MI FAMILIA AND IT IS PERFECTO!
END

"ONE LOUD'S TRASH..."

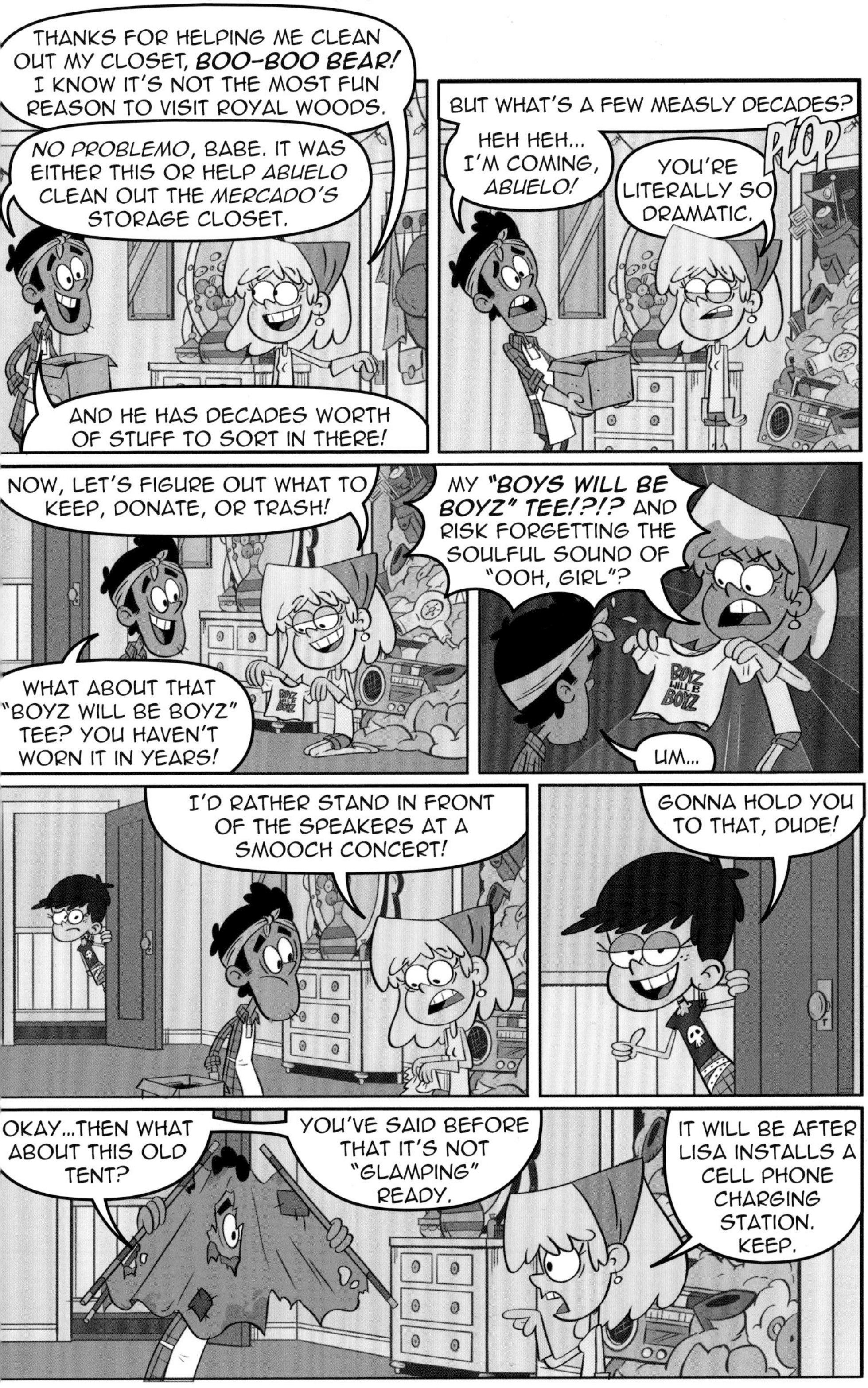
THANKS FOR HELPING ME CLEAN OUT MY CLOSET, BOO-BOO BEAR! I KNOW IT'S NOT THE MOST FUN REASON TO VISIT ROYAL WOODS.
NO PROBLEMO, BABE. IT WAS EITHER THIS OR HELP ABUELO CLEAN OUT THE MERCADO'S STORAGE CLOSET.
AND HE HAS DECADES WORTH OF STUFF TO SORT IN THERE!
BUT WHAT'S A FEW MEASLY DECADES?
HEH HEH... I'M COMING, ABUELO!
PLOP
YOU'RE LITERALLY SO DRAMATIC.
NOW, LET'S FIGURE OUT WHAT TO KEEP, DONATE, OR TRASH!
WHAT ABOUT THAT "BOYZ WILL BE BOYZ" TEE? YOU HAVEN'T WORN IT IN YEARS!
BOYZ WILL B BOYZ
MY "BOYS WILL BE BOYZ" TEE!?!? AND RISK FORGETTING THE SOULFUL SOUND OF "OOH, GIRL"?
UM...
I'D RATHER STAND IN FRONT OF THE SPEAKERS AT A SMOOCH CONCERT!
GONNA HOLD YOU TO THAT, DUDE!
OKAY...THEN WHAT ABOUT THIS OLD TENT?
YOU'VE SAID BEFORE THAT IT'S NOT "GLAMPING" READY.
IT WILL BE AFTER LISA INSTALLS A CELL PHONE CHARGING STATION. KEEP.

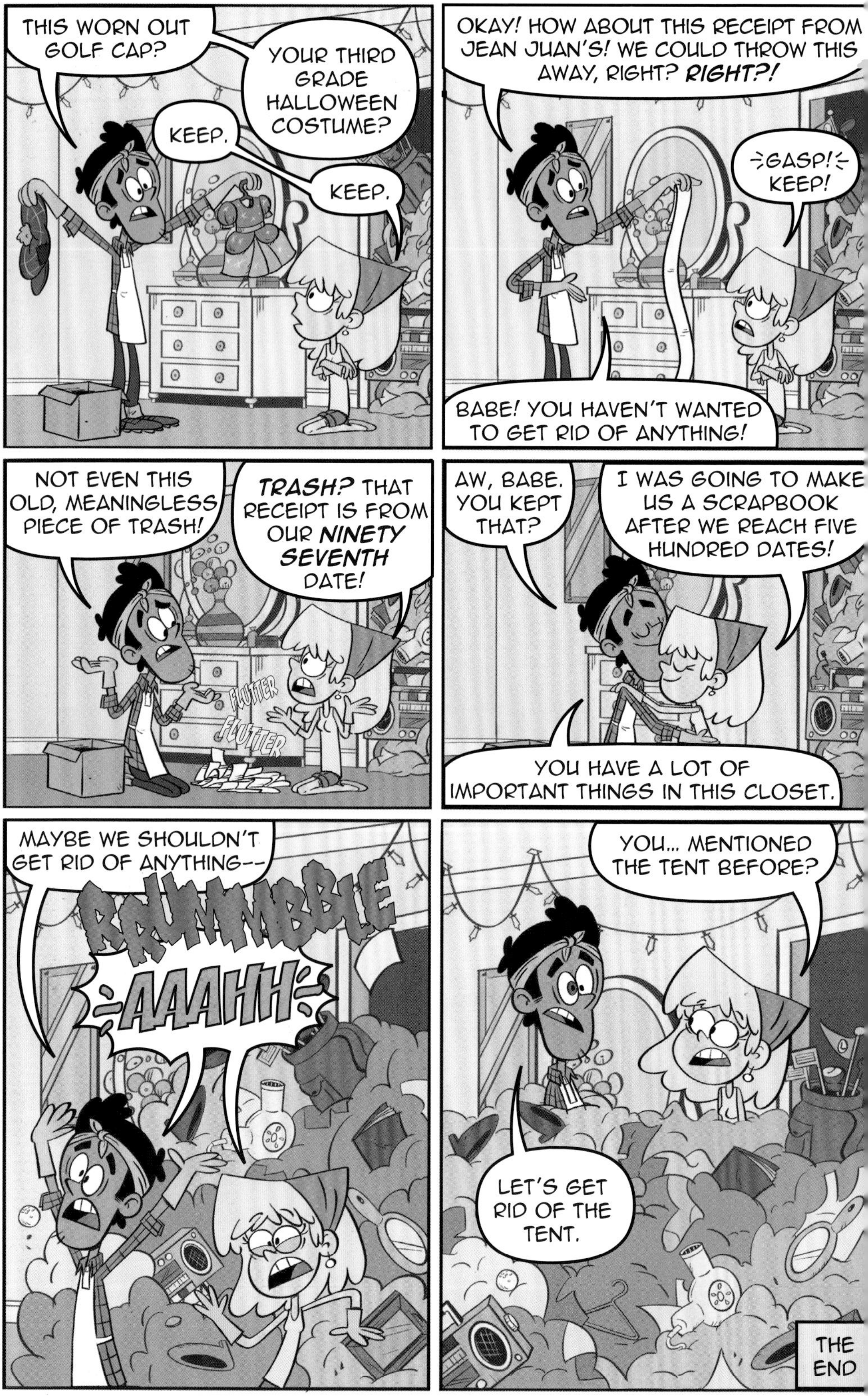
THIS WORN OUT GOLF CAP?
KEEP.
YOUR THIRD GRADE HALLOWEEN COSTUME?
KEEP.
OKAY! HOW ABOUT THIS RECEIPT FROM JEAN JUAN'S! WE COULD THROW THIS AWAY, RIGHT? RIGHT?!
GASP! KEEP!
BABE! YOU HAVEN'T WANTED TO GET RID OF ANYTHING!
NOT EVEN THIS OLD, MEANINGLESS PIECE OF TRASH!
TRASH? THAT RECEIPT IS FROM OUR NINETY SEVENTH DATE!
FLUTTER
FLUTTER
AW, BABE. YOU KEPT THAT?
I WAS GOING TO MAKE US A SCRAPBOOK AFTER WE REACH FIVE HUNDRED DATES!
YOU HAVE A LOT OF IMPORTANT THINGS IN THIS CLOSET.
MAYBE WE SHOULDN'T GET RID OF ANYTHING--
RRUMMBBLE
AAAHH
YOU... MENTIONED THE TENT BEFORE?
LET'S GET RID OF THE TENT.
THE END

"PREP TALK"

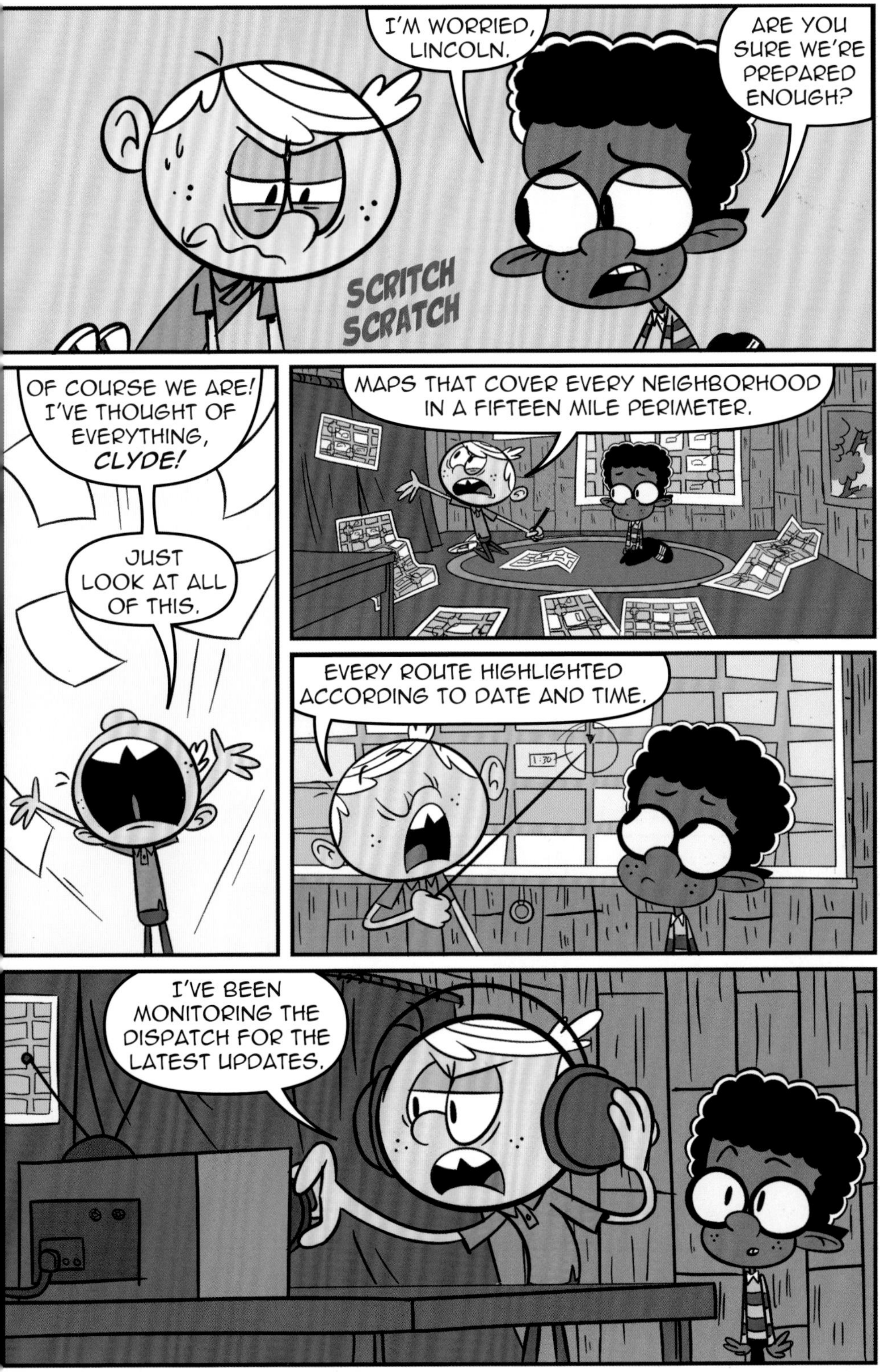
I'M WORRIED, LINCOLN.
ARE YOU SURE WE'RE PREPARED ENOUGH?
SCRITCH SCRATCH
OF COURSE WE ARE! I'VE THOUGHT OF EVERYTHING, CLYDE!
JUST LOOK AT ALL OF THIS.
MAPS THAT COVER EVERY NEIGHBORHOOD IN A FIFTEEN MILE PERIMETER.
EVERY ROUTE HIGHLIGHTED ACCORDING TO DATE AND TIME.
I'VE BEEN MONITORING THE DISPATCH FOR THE LATEST UPDATES.

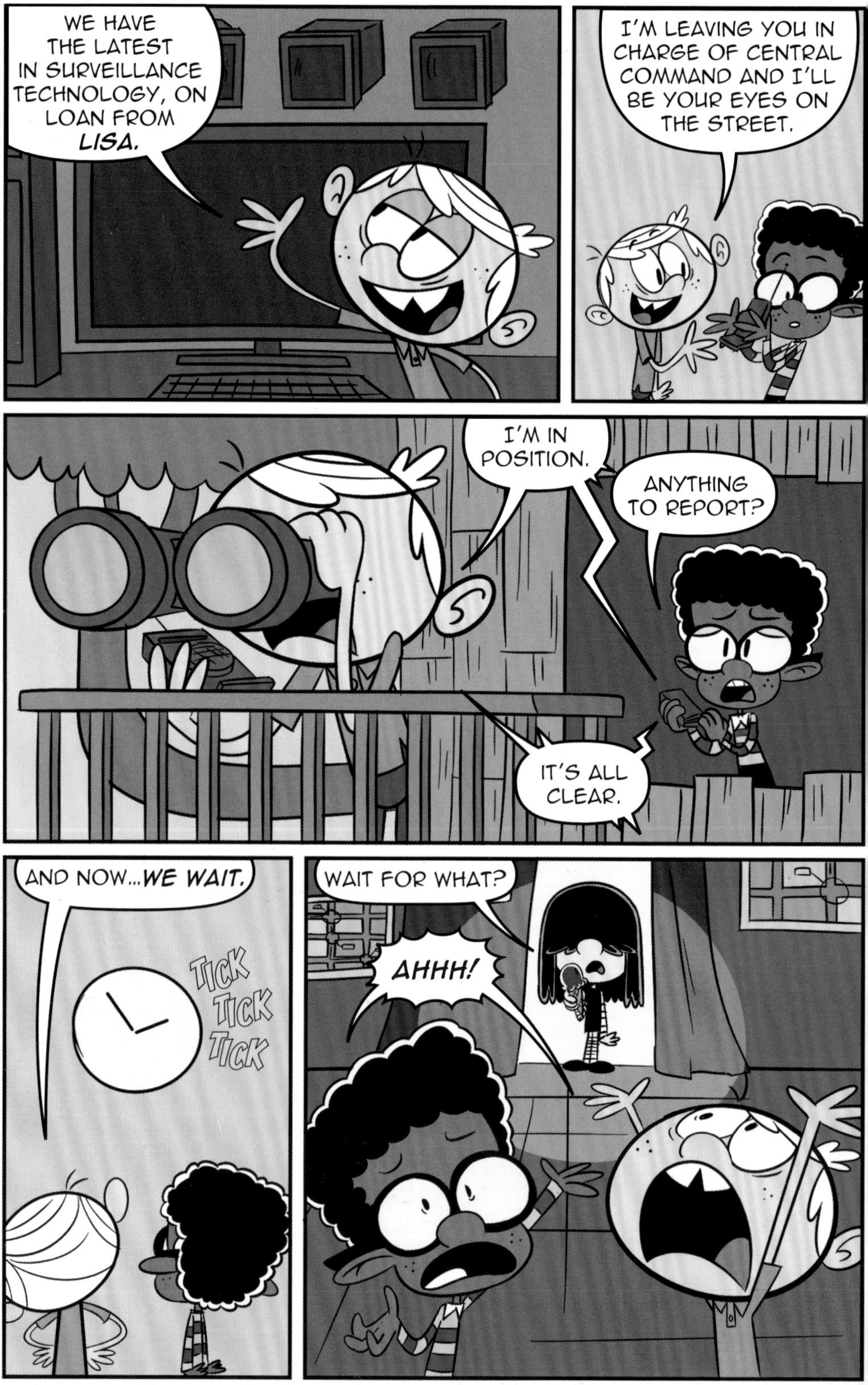
WE HAVE THE LATEST IN SURVEILLANCE TECHNOLOGY, ON LOAN FROM LISA.
I'M LEAVING YOU IN CHARGE OF CENTRAL COMMAND AND I'LL BE YOUR EYES ON THE STREET.
I'M IN POSITION.
ANYTHING TO REPORT?
IT'S ALL CLEAR.
AND NOW...WE WAIT.
TICK
TICK
TICK
WAIT FOR WHAT?
AHHH!

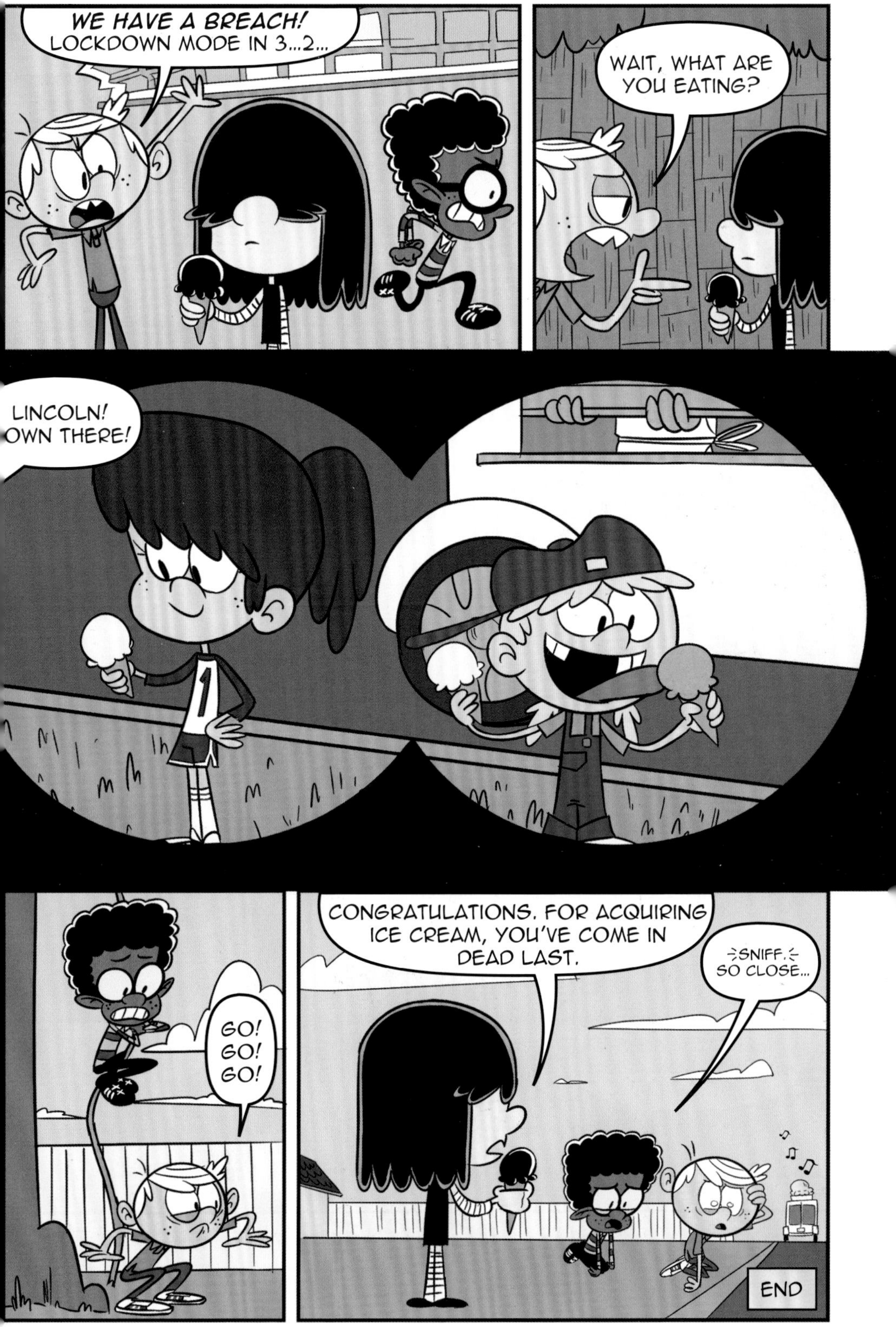
WE HAVE A BREACH! LOCKDOWN MODE IN 3...2...
WAIT, WHAT ARE YOU EATING?
LINCOLN! OWN THERE!
GO! GO! GO!
CONGRATULATIONS. FOR ACQUIRING ICE CREAM, YOU'VE COME IN DEAD LAST.
SNIFF. SO CLOSE...
END

"CASA CAMPERS"

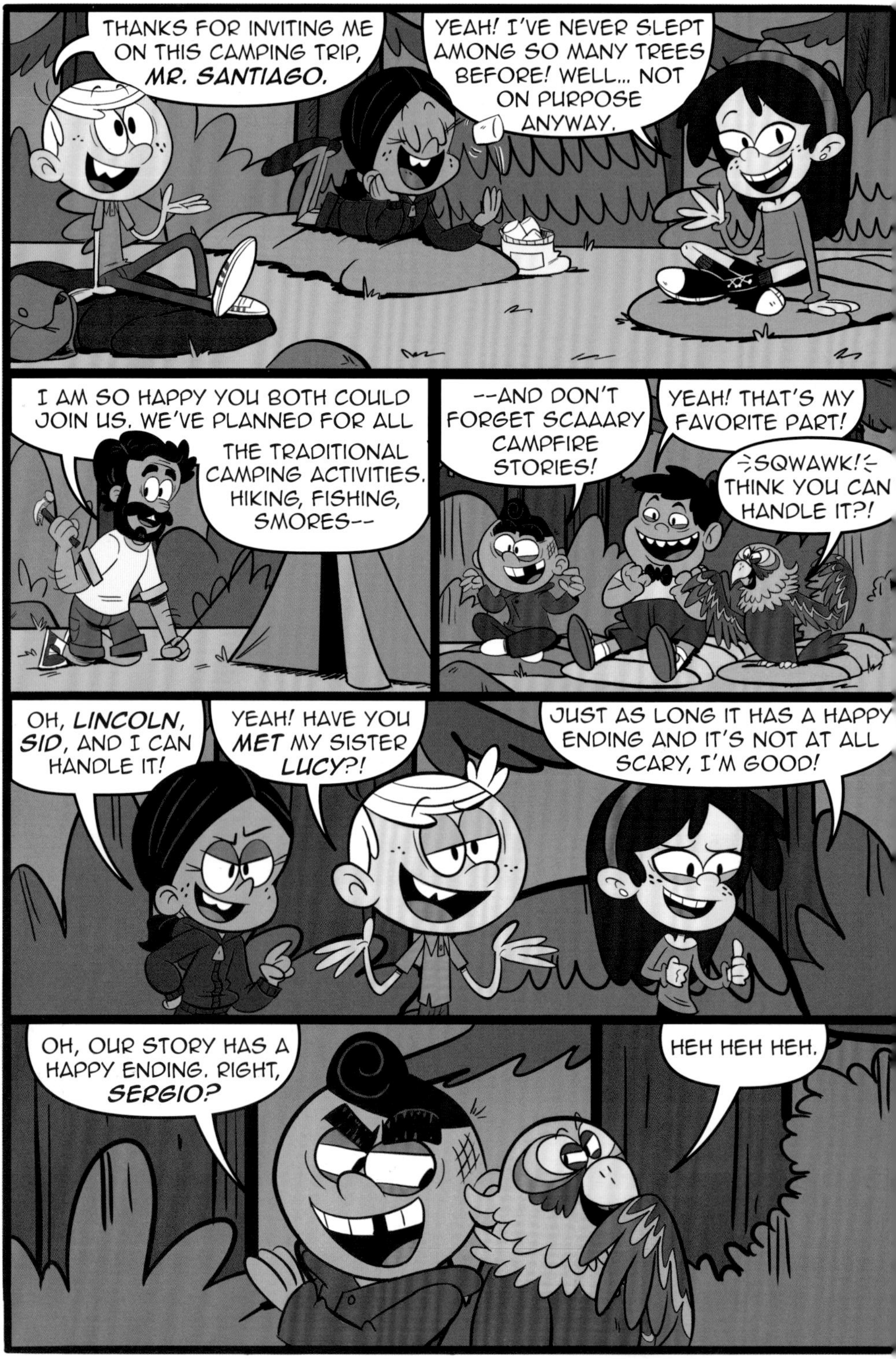
THANKS FOR INVITING ME ON THIS CAMPING TRIP, MR. SANTIAGO.
YEAH! I'VE NEVER SLEPT AMONG SO MANY TREES BEFORE! WELL... NOT ON PURPOSE ANYWAY.
I AM SO HAPPY YOU BOTH COULD JOIN US. WE'VE PLANNED FOR ALL
THE TRADITIONAL CAMPING ACTIVITIES. HIKING, FISHING, SMORES--
--AND DON'T FORGET SCAAARY CAMPFIRE STORIES!
YEAH! THAT'S MY FAVORITE PART!
SQWAWK! THINK YOU CAN HANDLE IT?!
OH, LINCOLN, SID, AND I CAN HANDLE IT!
YEAH! HAVE YOU MET MY SISTER LUCY?!
JUST AS LONG IT HAS A HAPPY ENDING AND IT'S NOT AT ALL SCARY, I'M GOOD!
OH, OUR STORY HAS A HAPPY ENDING. RIGHT, SERGIO?
HEH HEH HEH.

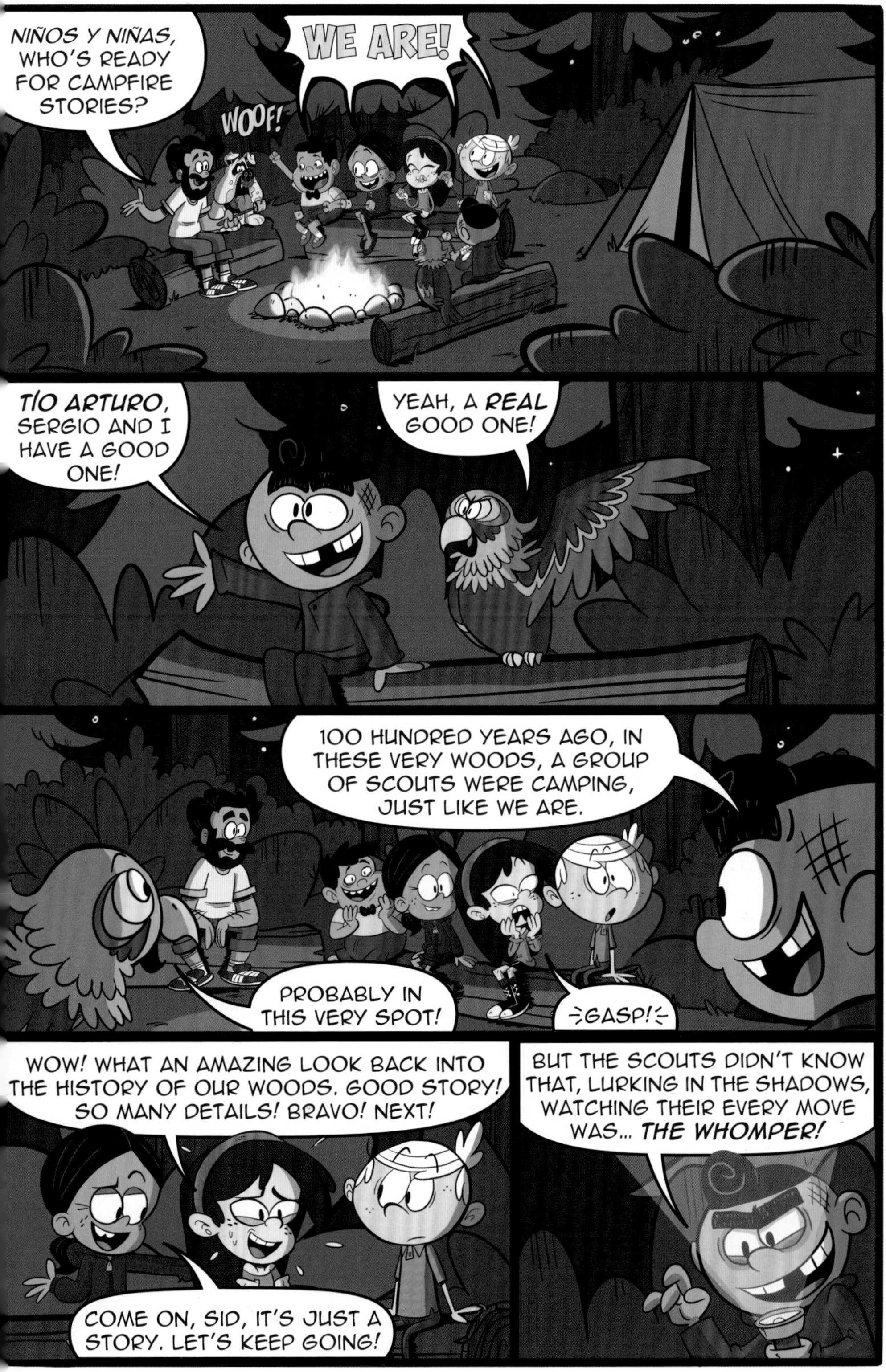
NIÑOS Y NIÑAS, WHO'S READY FOR CAMPFIRE STORIES?
WE ARE!
WOOF!
TÍO ARTURO, SERGIO AND I HAVE A GOOD ONE!
YEAH, A REAL GOOD ONE!
100 HUNDRED YEARS AGO, IN THESE VERY WOODS, A GROUP OF SCOUTS WERE CAMPING, JUST LIKE WE ARE.
PROBABLY IN THIS VERY SPOT!
GASP!
WOW! WHAT AN AMAZING LOOK BACK INTO THE HISTORY OF OUR WOODS. GOOD STORY! SO MANY DETAILS! BRAVO! NEXT!
COME ON, SID, IT'S JUST A STORY. LET'S KEEP GOING!
BUT THE SCOUTS DIDN'T KNOW THAT, LURKING IN THE SHADOWS, WATCHING THEIR EVERY MOVE WAS... THE WHOMPER!

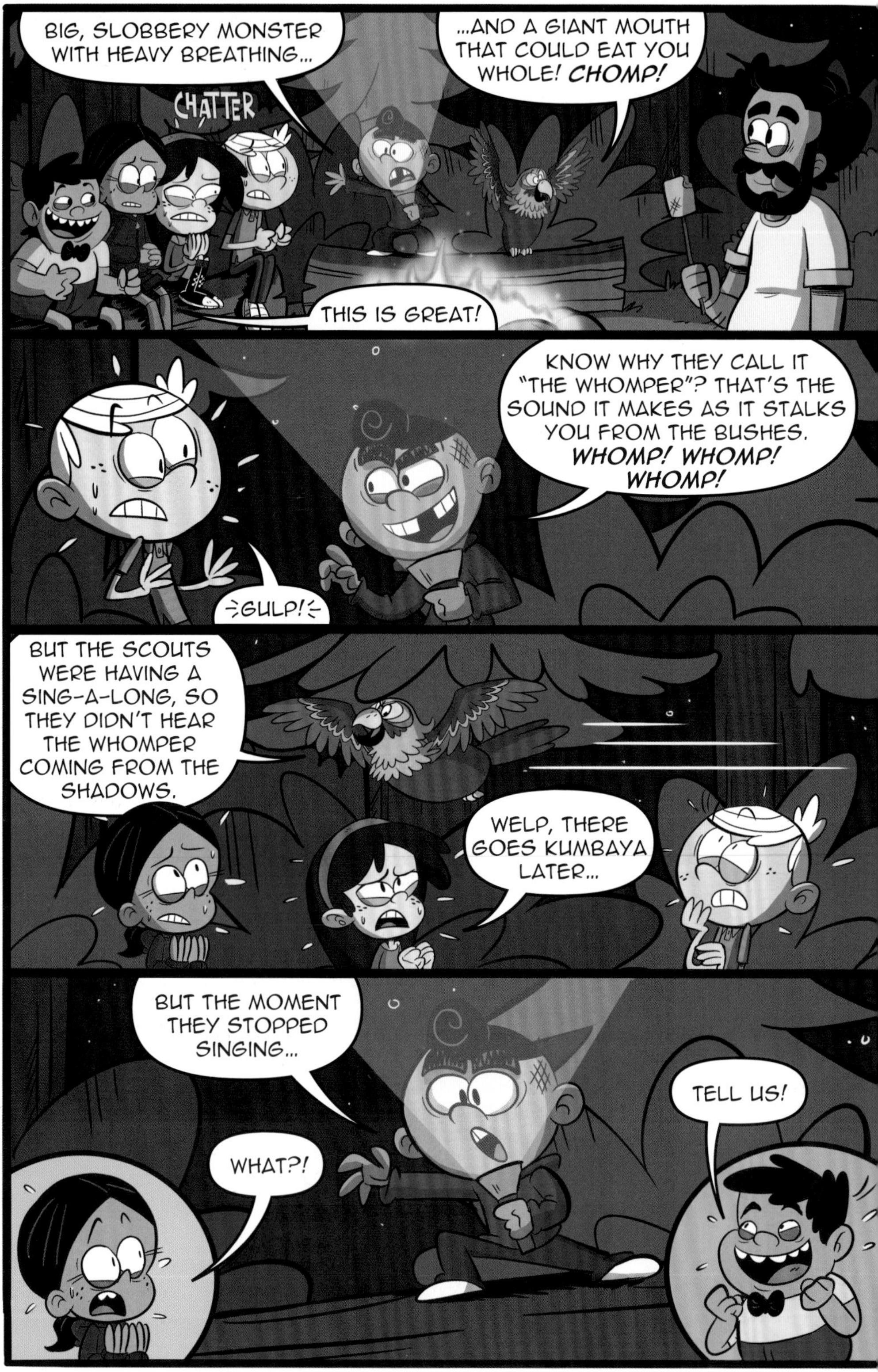
BIG, SLOBBERY MONSTER WITH HEAVY BREATHING...
...AND A GIANT MOUTH THAT COULD EAT YOU WHOLE! CHOMP!
CHATTER
THIS IS GREAT!
KNOW WHY THEY CALL IT "THE WHOMPER"? THAT'S THE SOUND IT MAKES AS IT STALKS YOU FROM THE BUSHES. WHOMP! WHOMP! WHOMP!
GULP!
BUT THE SCOUTS WERE HAVING A SING-A-LONG, SO THEY DIDN'T HEAR THE WHOMPER COMING FROM THE SHADOWS.
WELP, THERE GOES KUMBAYA LATER...
BUT THE MOMENT THEY STOPPED SINGING...
TELL US!
WHAT?!

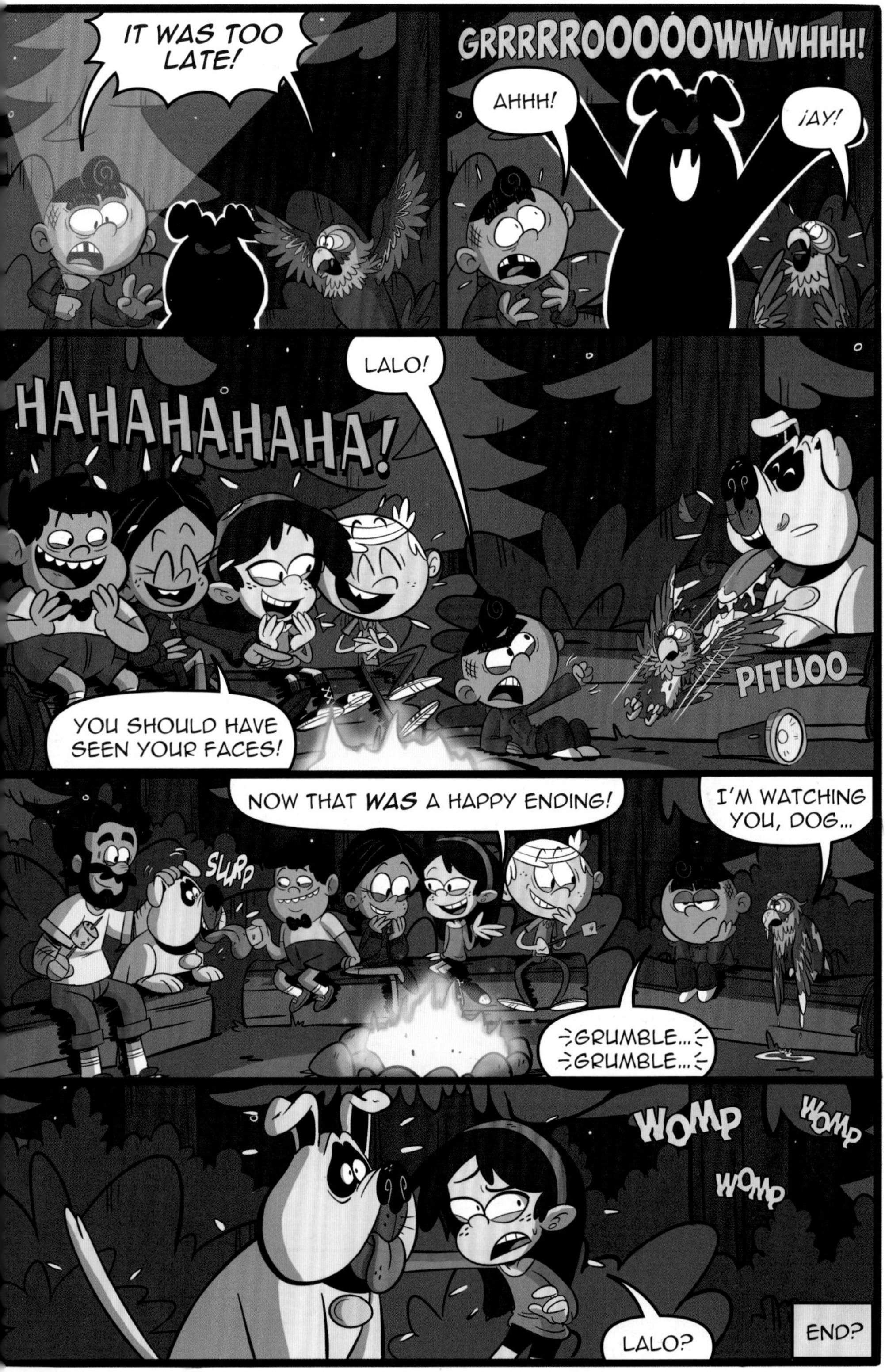
IT WAS TOO LATE!
GRRRRROOOOOWWWHHH!
AHHH!
¡AY!
HAHAHAHAHA!
LALO!
PITUOO
YOU SHOULD HAVE SEEN YOUR FACES!
SLURP
NOW THAT WAS A HAPPY ENDING!
I'M WATCHING YOU, DOG...
GRUMBLE... GRUMBLE...
WOMP
WOMP
WOMP
LALO?
END?

"POPSICLE PROBLEMS"

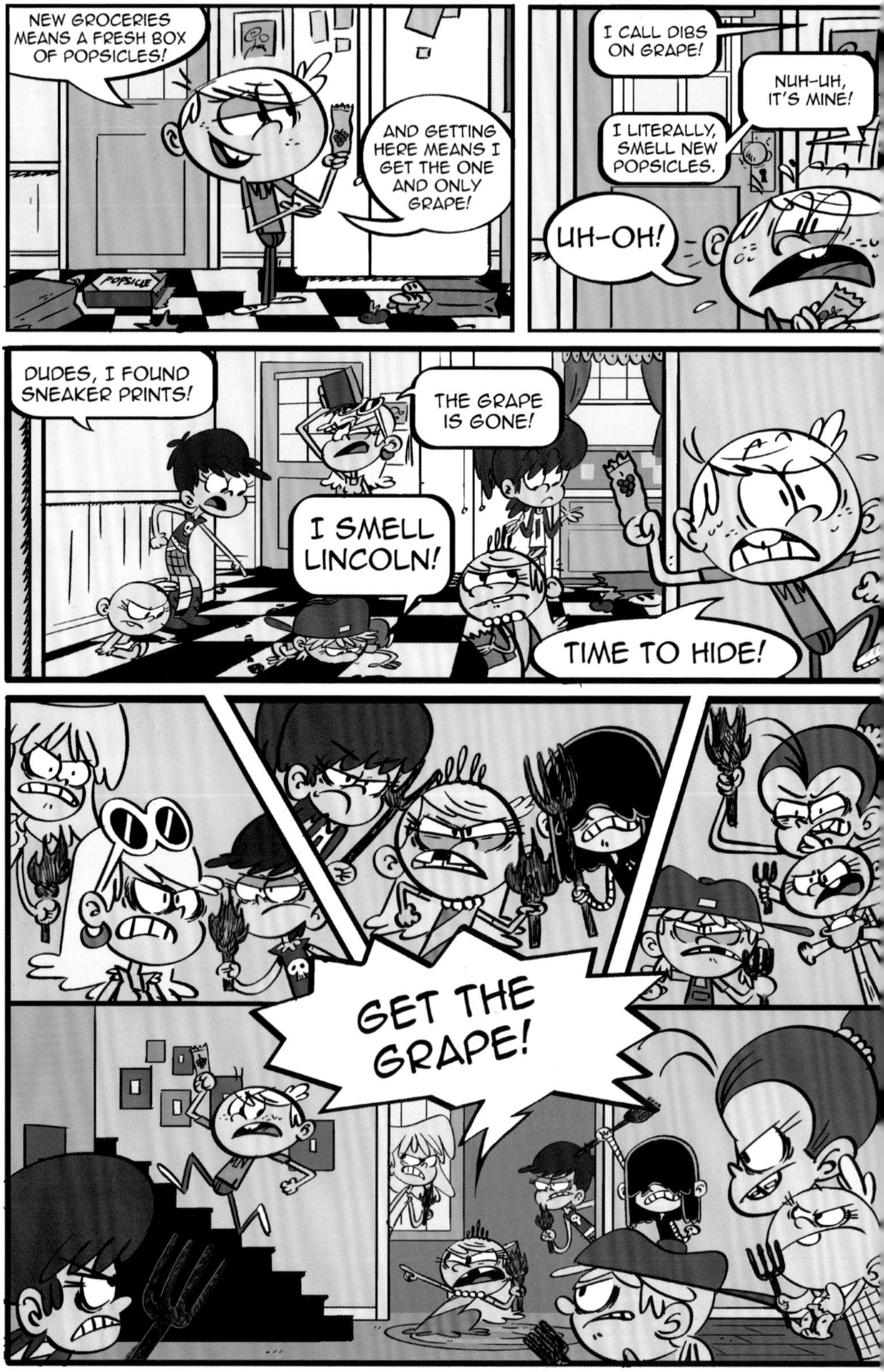
NEW GROCERIES MEANS A FRESH BOX OF POPSICLES!
AND GETTING HERE MEANS I GET THE ONE AND ONLY GRAPE!
POPSICLE
I CALL DIBS ON GRAPE!
NUH-UH, IT'S MINE!
I LITERALLY, SMELL NEW POPSICLES.
UH-OH!
DUDES, I FOUND SNEAKER PRINTS!
THE GRAPE IS GONE!
I SMELL LINCOLN!
TIME TO HIDE!
GET THE GRAPE!

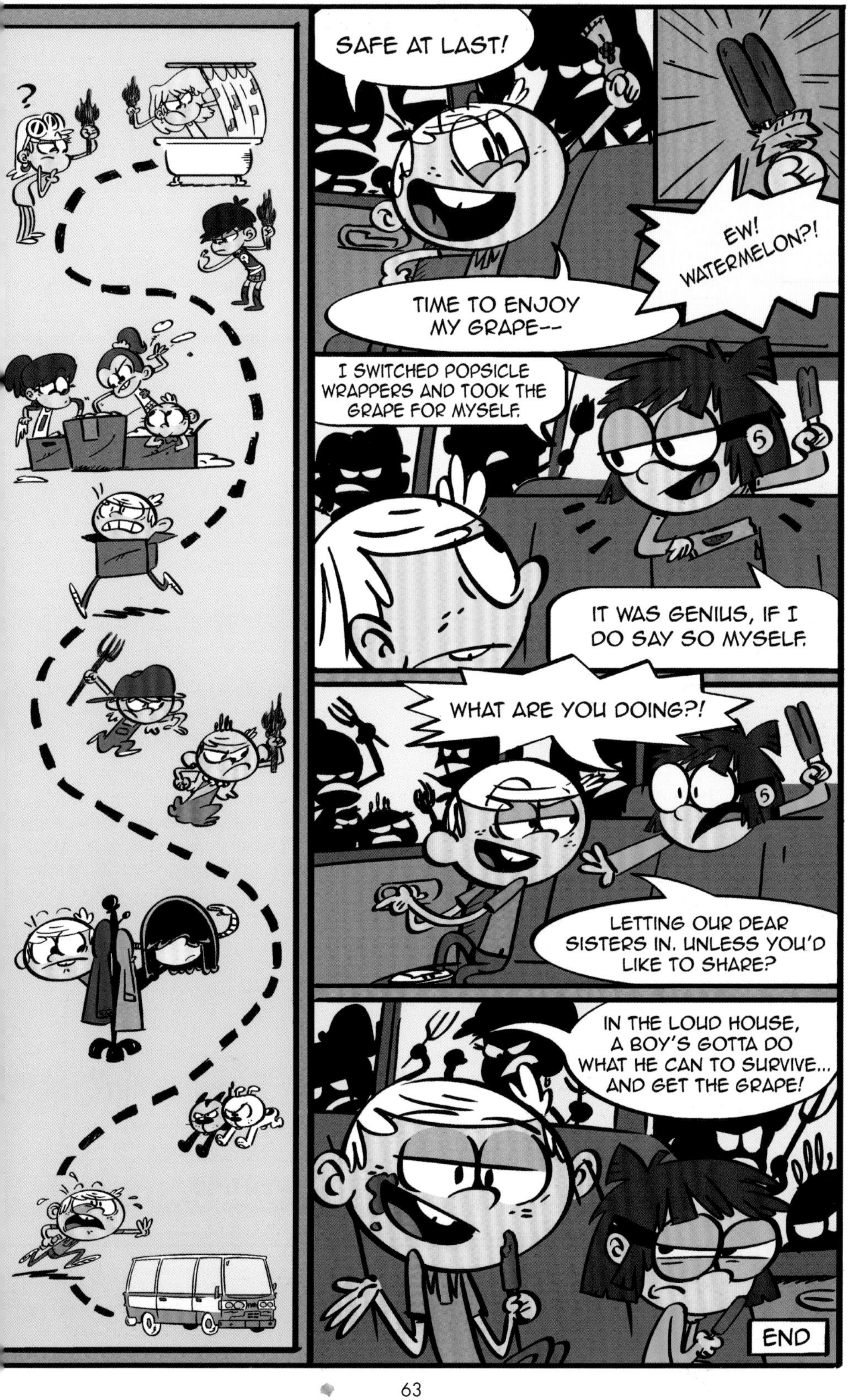
SAFE AT LAST!
TIME TO ENJOY MY GRAPE--
EW! WATERMELON?!
I SWITCHED POPSICLE WRAPPERS AND TOOK THE GRAPE FOR MYSELF.
IT WAS GENIUS, IF I DO SAY SO MYSELF.
WHAT ARE YOU DOING?!
LETTING OUR DEAR SISTERS IN. UNLESS YOU'D LIKE TO SHARE?
IN THE LOUD HOUSE, A BOY'S GOTTA DO WHAT HE CAN TO SURVIVE... AND GET THE GRAPE!
END

WATCH OUT FOR PAPERCUTZ

Welcome to the very first THE LOUD HOUSE SUMMER SPECIAL from Papercutz — those bashful beachgoer dedicated to publishing great graphic novels for all ages. I'm Jim Salicrup, Editor-in-Chief and all-natural sun-blocke here to cap off this Loud summer-celebration with some silly quiz to find out which Loud sibling you're most lik during the summer…

Summer certainly is a special season. Countless students eagerly await summer, not just for the many pleasures the season brings, but because it means school's out. Unless they've been assigned to…>choke!< >gasp!< Summer School. Fortunately, Lincoln Loud and his sisters didn't have to attend any summer classes and were free to enjoy the summer to the fullest, as we've just seen. The question is, which Loud is the most like you when it comes to having summer fun. Is it…

LINCOLN — who has more time to spend with his friend Clyde, catch up on his favorite comicbooks, play video games, watch TV, head out with his family to the beach, go camping with Ronnie Anne and Sid, and so much more? Except for when it ends, there's almost nothing about summer Lincoln doesn't like.

Or are you like…

LORI — While Lori is interested in maintaining her long-distance relationship with Bobby year 'round, the summer does provide some unique problems. Not only is Bobby still busy helping his family at the *Mercado*, but he also takes on summer jobs, such as being a lifeguard at community pools. Fortunately, hanging out at pools is rather fun, providing ample time for tanning and swimming. A lot nicer for Lori than hanging out at the *Mercado*.

LENI — Each season demands countless wardrobe decisions from this fashion-conscious gal. And with so many summer activities (not to mention working at the mall with Fiona and Miguel), she may spend almost as much time deciding, and even creating, what to wear.

LUNA — This is the season of big outdoor rock concerts and festivals. Luna, along with Sam, will be rocking around the clock all summer either catching their favorite bands perform or making music together in their band.

LUAN — The main virtue of summer for this stand-up comedian is the free time to spend polishing up her act — writing new gags and testing them out on her family. Ultimately, comics are night people, so a season centered around the sun isn't as appealing to Luan and Mr. Coconuts.

LYNN — While active every season, having time off from school allows athletic Lynn the opportunity to go all-out with outdoor sports. This is a great relief to her family, as they no longer need to stay out of her way when she's practicing sports indoors.

LUCY — Perhaps the least Summery Loud, her favorite season is Autumn, when leaves are dying. While others may despair when rain destroys the possibility of a day at the beach, Lucy, who likes to despair, welcomes all forms of gloom.

LOLA — What beauty queen doesn't love th opportunity to bask in the sun while wearing a new swimsuit and designer sunglasses?

LANA — This girl loves to get down and dirty, literall (as Lori would say). Who else would dumpster dive wit a pet possum?

LISA — While mostly content to remain in her lab she will venture outdoors, usually to conduct cover experiments on her siblings. But then again, isn't life itse one big experiment to Lisa?

LILY — With far less life experience than anyone else i her family, Lily is still learning exactly what the season are.

Which Loud are you most like in the summer? I thin I'm a cross between Luan and Lisa. Then again, I'm also little like Lincoln and I'm looking forward to all sorts c comics, especially…

THE CASAGRANDES #1 "We're All Familia available now, it's a special graphic novel featuring new Casagrandes stories as well as a few favorites that wer featured in THE LOUD HOUSE graphic novels. As special added bonus for the premiere volume of TH CASAGRANDES, we're featuring three exclusive min interviews with a few of the real live talents behin the Nickelodeon show: Co-Executive Producer Migue Puga, Consulting Producer and Cultural Consultar Lalo Alcaraz, and the voice of Ronnie Anne, Izabell Alvarez. I was thrilled to have the opportunity to as them questions which they so generously took the tim to answer.

Of course, I'm still looking forward to the upcomin graphic novels featuring our other favorite Nickelodeo series, as well. After all, THE LOUD HOUSE graphi novels are always in season.

Thanks,

Jim

STAY IN TOUCH!

EMAIL: salicrup@papercutz.com
WEB: papercutz.com
TWITTER: @papercutzgn
INSTAGRAM: @papercutzgn
FACEBOOK: PAPERCUTZGRAPHICNOVELS
FANMAIL: Papercutz, 160 Broadway, Suite 700 East Wing, New York, NY 10038

Go to papercutz.com and sign up for the free Papercutz e-newslette